ALL BARK, NO BITE

by Kara Emily Krantz

ALL BARK, NO BITE

SPECIAL NOTE

Anyone receiving permission to produce ALL BARK, NO BITE is required to give credit to the Author as sole and exclusive Author of the Play on the title page of all programs distributed in connection with performances of the Play and in all instances in which the title of the Play appears for purposes of advertising, publicizing or otherwise exploiting the Play and/or a production thereof. The name of the Author must appear on a separate line, in which no other name appears, immediately beneath the title and in size of type equal to 50% of the size of the largest, most prominent letter used for the title of the Play. No person, firm, or entity may receive credit larger or more prominent than that accorded the Author.

SPECIAL NOTE ON SONGS AND RECORDINGS

For performances of copyrighted songs, arrangements or recordings mentioned in these Plays, the permission of the copyright owner(s) must be obtained. Other songs, arrangements or recordings may be substituted provided permission from the copyright owner(s) of such songs, arrangements or recordings is obtained; or songs, arrangements or recordings in the public domain may be substituted.

Cover Art Design: Barron Henzel
Book Design: Jonathan Cook
First Edition: March 2024
ISBN 978-1-7375216-9-3

To my furry friends who have taught me so much about life (and love): Kash, Quinn, and Levi

To my mentor in theater, directing, and the dedicated exploration of our most authentic lives: Diana Canterbury

To my childhood bestie, Jessica Ralph, who has always supported my whimsical ways and given excellent counsel/input through the many revisions of this play. This story would not be what it is without her.

And to the many friends and family who have supported ALL BARK, NO BITE's (and my) journey over the years. I would not be who I am without you.

Cardigans and cardamom! Thank you and enjoy.

"I've seen a look in dogs' eyes, a quickly vanishing look of amazed contempt, and I am convinced that basically dogs think humans are nuts." - John Steinbeck

"My little dog - a heartbeat at my feet." - Edith Wharton

ALL BARK, NO BITE by Kara Emily Krantz had a fully produced workshop at Singh Performance Center in Whitinsville, MA in June 2016. It was produced by Becoming More Productions with director Kara Emily Krantz; stage manager Cassie Tortorici; asst. stage manager Dana Fitzpatrick; and technical director Dave Plante. The cast was as follows:

EUGENE .... Wade Porter
CHARLOTTE .... Vivian Nichols
ROBERT .... Sean Costello
BELLA .... Michelle England
SUZANNE .... Peter Arsenault

ALL BARK, NO BITE by Kara Emily Krantz had its World Premiere at Calliope Theater in Boylston, MA in February 2019. It was produced by Calliope Productions with director Kara Emily Krantz; stage manager Lorraine Hruska; asst. stage manager Olivia Lyerly; and technical director Dave Ludt. The cast was as follows:

EUGENE .... John Goodale
CHARLOTTE .... Julianne McGourty
ROBERT .... Ian Dowell
BELLA .... Meg Norton
SUZANNE .... Michael Pray

ALL BARK, NO BITE

CHARACTERS

EUGENE
Male-presenting, canine (unspecified breed), any age (preferably older, but not necessary); intelligent, superior, with a sarcastic, dry wit. Set in his ways.

CHARLOTTE
Female, 20-50; kind, hard-working architect with a gentle, patient nature and particular, nervous tendencies. Set in her ways.

ROBERT
Male, 20-60; a tolerably good guy, he enjoys his life and has an enduringly upbeat attitude.

BELLA
Female, canine (Maltese puppy), any age (preferably younger); happy, enthusiastic, loves attention, and could charm the lolli off a pop.

SUZANNE
Any gender (leans female-presenting and/or transfemme), any age; Charlotte's neighbor: nosy, a bit abrasive, and in the midst of an emotional/physical/spiritual transition; sincerely cares for and protects Charlotte. A penchant for being extra. Not a dog lover.

PLACE
Living room: an organized, comfortable condominium in the suburbs.

TIME
Present Day.

AUTHOR'S NOTES

HUMANS AS DOGS:
The intention for the canine characters (Eugene and Bella) is two-fold: 1) for the dogs to understand the humans, but the humans not to understand the dogs and 2) to be played as essentially human with touches of canine quirkiness.

Charlotte and Robert should not speak to their dogs with condescension or use too much "baby talk."

***By No Means** should Eugene and Bella: wear animal costumes (including ears/tails, furry/fuzzy items or clothes), crawl on all fours, sit on typical dog beds, or sniff derrières.

The human-as-dog conceit unfolds throughout the top of the show. In production, the average audience member has their "ah-ha" moment when Charlotte delivers Eugene's water dish (p.15). Prior to that, viewers are intrigued as to the nature of Eugene and Charlotte's relationship, and it is a source of delight when they fully realize: "OMG - he's a dog!"

By Bella's arrival, the conceit is universally accepted.

To this effect, the playwright requests for marketing materials and actors (as much as possible) to please not reveal the human-as-dog conceit.

SUZANNE:
Suzanne's humor should be primarily derived from her personality rather than her gender, sex, or physical representation/appearance.

Furthermore, Suzanne's alcohol drinking serves as an aid to her characterization and candor, but we should always (audibly) understand her and she should not get sloppy or messy.

That said, have a heckuvalotta fun!

<u>ACT ONE</u>

Eugene sits on the center cushion of a couch, wearing argyle. He waits. Looks around. Tired of waiting, he clears his throat.

CHARLOTTE. *(Offstage, frazzled.)* I'll be there in a minute, Eugene!

EUGENE. Yes, well, take your time. I am a master of the endurance of monotony. *(Endures; spots newspaper.)* Did we finish the crossword today, Charlotte? Perhaps I should check-

CHARLOTTE. *(Offstage.)* Oh my God!

EUGENE. Please, let us reserve such exclamations for our bedtime prayers. Everything all right, Charlotte? *(Eugene listens; no response. Shrugs; reclines. Charlotte enters from hallway, holding a pregnancy stick. Eugene does not see her.)*

CHARLOTTE. This can't be happening right now.

EUGENE. I was not lying on the couch! *(Charlotte exits to kitchen.)* Charlotte, would you please fetch me some tea? *(Attempts to focus; can't.)* Life is exceedingly tiresome without you. Please come back and sit with me! *(Dishes clatter in kitchen.)* Charlotte, are you all right?

CHARLOTTE. *(Offstage.)* I'm fine, Eugene! Don't worry! Just prepping for dinner and I'm totally, completely fine! Stay where you are! *(Eugene approaches the kitchen door. A clatter, a shriek; he enters the kitchen.)* Get out of the kitchen! *(Eugene retreats, remains by kitchen door. Charlotte enters wearing an apron, pregnancy stick in hand; she stuffs it in her apron pocket before Eugene sees.)* Eugene.

EUGENE. Charlotte.

CHARLOTTE. What are you doing?

EUGENE. Not going in the kitchen, that's for sure.

CHARLOTTE. *(Tidying up the already spotless room.)* You know, I love you, but you're very strange. I'm sorry for yelling, but you know I don't like anyone in the kitchen while I'm cooking.

EUGENE. Won't happen again. Charlotte, I was hoping we could-

CHARLOTTE. Oh, this can't be happening- not today, not with Robert finally ... it's just a big night for us, Eugene, that's all I'm saying. It was already a big night, I was already kinda freaking out - but now? Now?!

EUGENE. Yes, I find this all ... quite perplexing.

CHARLOTTE. Who knows what'll happen now! And not knowing what to expect, Eugene, is almost always a precursor to generalized anxiety, you know? You know what I'm saying? Generally? Yes? Oh gosh, he'll be here soon. What am I going to say?

EUGENE. You'll say, "Why, hello, Robert. How splendid to see you this evening, much as we do every Friday night."

CHARLOTTE. Tonight is a very special night, Eugene!

EUGENE. I'm not trying to argue with you, Charlotte.

CHARLOTTE. And to think, we were going to surprise you! How ridiculous is that?

EUGENE. I don't like surprises, Charlotte.

CHARLOTTE. Whatever, shake it off.

EUGENE. You already know this about me, Charlotte.

CHARLOTTE. Here, let me fix your sweater. Is it itchy? Are you comfortable?

EUGENE. Stop fussing with me!

CHARLOTTE. You know what? Actually, this could be good. 'Cuz, I mean, everything so far has been great. Robert is really great. He's funny and strong and smart -

EUGENE. *(Snorts.)* Smart?

CHARLOTTE. He's considerate, and kind - he treats me very well - even you, for that matter.

EUGENE. Yes, it's been a real fairytale.

CHARLOTTE. He's always looking out for us. And he consistently reminds me I can do anything I put my mind to.

EUGENE. Yes, because it's healthy to have unrealistic expectations for one's life.

CHARLOTTE. And he's got that smile that just flips your heart. Robert's a good guy; a really great guy.

EUGENE. Robert is tolerable.

CHARLOTTE. He has some exceptionally fine qualities.

EUGENE. Robert is somewhat tolerable.

CHARLOTTE. I mean, you like him, don't you, Eugie?

EUGENE. I just said he's tolerable! Why must you keep pressing me?

CHARLOTTE. Come here, Eugene. *(Charlotte gestures beside her; Eugene sits.)* I want you to understand something.

EUGENE. I was trying to be agreeable.

CHARLOTTE. It's important to me that you like him. It's important to me that you're happy. Gosh, I wish I knew how you really felt.

EUGENE. Well, in that case, Charlotte - not a huge fan.

CHARLOTTE. But whatever happens, today is a step forward.

EUGENE. And I'd prefer if we never saw him again.

CHARLOTTE. You're still my favorite guy, Eugene.

EUGENE. How comforting. Look at me, I'm comforted. *(Charlotte pats his head.)* Yes, ignore my advice but pat my head.

CHARLOTTE. I appreciate your patience, Eugie. And I'm sorry I yelled at you. I've read that if I feel nervous, it makes you feel nervous, too.

EUGENE. I would like to believe I have a more resilient sense of identity than that.

CHARLOTTE. You know, like, feeding off my emotions. Absorbing them and reflecting them back. Aw, you're like a little reflection of me! But I shouldn't have yelled at you. Oh gosh, he'll be here any second. Do I look all right? *(She notices her apron; removes it, drapes it over the couch.)*

EUGENE. I think you look smashing -

CHARLOTTE. Maybe I should dress up more. Perhaps we're getting too comfortable, and he's like, totally unimpressed. Oh gosh, the air is like trapping in my chest and running across my skin and I'm dizzy and you're adorable and I can't breathe and if I can't breathe I can't talk to him and we need to have a serious conversation!

EUGENE. Ah! I refuse to feed off this! Like an emotional leech without a strong enough sense of self! *(Meditates.)* I am calm; I am at peace.

CHARLOTTE. Maybe bringing her here is a mistake. Maybe all of this was a mistake. *(Clutches Eugene.)* Oh God, Eugene, what if this is the end of everything we know to be beautiful?

EUGENE. You're freaking me out! Do your calmy-breathing thing so we can cease operating from this negative energy space. *(Charlotte walks to the back of the couch, falls backwards over it. Eugne scurries to join her.)* Yes, that thing.

CHARLOTTE. In, out. Everything is okay. Everything is sunshine.

EUGENE. Everything looks like bad track lighting from here.

CHARLOTTE. In, out.

EUGENE. *(Looks at Charlotte.)* Fortunately, I find you adorable.

CHARLOTTE. In, out. I love you, Eugene.

EUGENE. Yes. That, too.

CHARLOTTE. No matter what, Eugie, we're gonna be okay. I'll always take care of you. *(She reaches for Eugene's hand.)*

EUGENE. And I you. *(Their moment is interrupted by a knock at the door. They disembark the couch; Charlotte straightens up, hangs her apron on a hook.)*

CHARLOTTE. Okay, he's here. He's here. He's here. *(She positions Eugene by the kitchen door.)* You look adorable in your argyle, by the way.

EUGENE. I look like a nincompoop.

CHARLOTTE. You're just the sweetest thing, you know that? The sweetest, most handsomest guy I know.

EUGENE. This both flatters and alarms me.

CHARLOTTE. You excited?

EUGENE. Positively beside myself.

CHARLOTTE. Stay there. *(Another knock at the door.)*

EUGENE. Go away!

CHARLOTTE. Shush, Eugene. Coming, Robert! *(She opens the door; Robert enters the room carrying a plant. He's pumped.)*

ROBERT. Here we go, tonight's the night! She's in the car, she's fine, she's good - she's got a blankie, all snuggled up. How we doing in here? Eugene primed; is he pumped? I'm pumped! *(Charlotte chuckles, taps her cheek. Robert obliges.)* Oh, hey. Sorry, I'm all over the place, I'm so excited. You look beautiful.

CHARLOTTE. Aren't you nervous?

ROBERT. I'm never nervous. *(He hands Charlotte the plant.)*

CHARLOTTE. Okay. Well, thank you, for this ... this shrubbery. I'll just put it over ... here. *(Near Eugene, who is horrified.)*

EUGENE. And what is this?

CHARLOTTE. You know, Robert ... if it's not the right time, we don't have to force it.

ROBERT. Of course it's the right time; why wouldn't it be? I've been looking forward to this all week. Heck, all my life. God, you really do look beautiful.

EUGENE. Excuse me, but do I have a say in any of this? I mean, of course you look beautiful- positively glowing- but about the other stuff. Most pressingly, what is this sad looking foliage doing in our abode, intruding -

ROBERT. Well hello, Eugene!

EUGENE. - intruding upon our space? And who in Cleopatra's name is in the car?

ROBERT. Well, don't you look cute?

EUGENE. *(Aghast.)* Cute?! *(He stomps away to his toy chest.)*

CHARLOTTE. Isn't he the best?

ROBERT. Sure. Definitely. Definitely the best. You're the best, dude!

EUGENE. *(Mocking Robert.)* You're the best, dude!

ROBERT. Is he feeling all right?

CHARLOTTE. Eugene? Yeah, he's fine. Maybe he's nervous. I'm not gonna lie, I feel a little sick ... about it, them, meeting. Maybe there's a reason we put this off.

ROBERT. Hey, it's only been two months, so we put it off two months, and that ain't bad. You had the Dorsey project all over the place, and I get it, you didn't need Bella messing things up. Hey, hun, you do look a little pale.

CHARLOTTE. It's pretty selfish, you know - everything always about us, us, us. Maybe they should've met like right when you met her, to see if they gel, if they blend.

ROBERT. They'll gel fine. They be gellin'.

EUGENE. Nobody talks like that.

CHARLOTTE. I mean, forget about Eugene, what if she doesn't like me? Here you've been bonding with her this whole time, but who am I? Maybe we've been avoiding this because we know it'll go terribly wrong and everything we've come to love about our lives will be ruined?

ROBERT. What? Whoa, Charlotte, you're acting very strange.

CHARLOTTE. Am I?

EUGENE. You do seem at an extra high frequency today.

CHARLOTTE. I mean, look at you - you're the one carrying random shrubs around.

EUGENE. Please remove that thing immediately.

ROBERT. Well, my mom always said first you should get a plant, then a dog, then you're ready to have a kid. Not that I'm saying we're ready to have a kid- God, no, but I figured, you know, we could handle the plant.

CHARLOTTE. *(Looks at the plant, attempts a smile.)* Okay.

ROBERT. Don't wanna skip too many steps, y'know.

CHARLOTTE. Okay.

ROBERT. Charlotte, is this about Bella? Is tonight some sort of make it/break it deal for you?

CHARLOTTE. Robert, no …

ROBERT. 'Cuz I'd really like to know what I'm getting myself into. Like a heads up.

CHARLOTTE. I'm not gonna blindside you; not like that. Here, sit with me for a sec. *(She pats beside her; Eugene jumps forward but realizes she didn't mean him. Robert sits.)* Robert, do you think we're moving too fast?

ROBERT. Um, okay.

CHARLOTTE. I just thought maybe you'd want to spend more time with her, before we like, integrate.

ROBERT. So this <u>is</u> about Bella.

CHARLOTTE. No, no. I just wondered -

ROBERT. Because I wanted you to meet months ago.

CHARLOTTE. I know, but I had work blueprints everywhere, and the mockups, and Eugene and I just got our space back -

ROBERT. No, I get all that. I just thought once the project wrapped up we would, you know, that maybe we could even ... Charlotte, do you ever want to meet Bella?

CHARLOTTE. Of course I do, it's just that -

ROBERT. Because I really thought tonight was the night.

CHARLOTTE. It was! It is, it totally still can be. I guess I'm just saying maybe I was wrong, maybe it would've been nice to spend time together ... like, all together, if that's, you know, the ultimate goal. All of us. Together.

ROBERT. Ah, I'm picking up what you're putting down.

EUGENE. Nobody talks like that.

CHARLOTTE. And then maybe Eugene wouldn't be so lonely.

EUGENE. Excuse me?

CHARLOTTE. I mean, look at him. He could really use a friend. *(Eugene gestures to himself in disbelief.)*

ROBERT. That's true. Hey, I get that you're nervous. But tonight's gonna be great, so let's focus on all the greatness.

CHARLOTTE. I think you're pretty great.

ROBERT. Well, I think you're super great.

CHARLOTTE. Thank you for talking this through with me.

EUGENE. No one is talking about anything! It's all a bunch of mumbo jumbo hooey-pooey. *(Mocking.)* "You're great - no, you're super, super great-"

ROBERT. Okay, hey, you know that time you ran out of spray glue for that ... the damn pillar column building -

CHARLOTTE. The library?

ROBERT. Yeah, and you needed the model for Jacqui the next day -

CHARLOTTE. Oh man, she would've killed me -

ROBERT. How long did we drive around looking for that stuff?

CHARLOTTE. I don't remember.

ROBERT. It was at least a tank of gas, Charlotte - middle of the night, trying to beat the time zones to find the right store, the right spray -

CHARLOTTE. Quality matters, Robert.

ROBERT. I know, I know, and of course that didn't work, all the stores were closed. But what did we do? We came home and we googled that shit and we shellacked the whole damn thing with hairspray -

CHARLOTTE. So much hairspray ...

ROBERT. But you and Jacqui still got your project, and Eugene got high off the fumes -

EUGENE. Mmmm, hairspray.

ROBERT. And what did I get, may you ask? I got five hours of driving around in a Beemer with a quality woman. I got a night of falling in love with a lady who needs a very specific adhesive spray in the middle of the night, and that's okay, because ... spray or not, I'm stuck on you.

CHARLOTTE. Oh Robert ... come here ... *(Robert pulls Charlotte close.)*

EUGENE. This is revolting.

ROBERT. I'm stuck on you, Charlotte Hastings. *(He goes to kiss her; Eugene starts gagging; Charlotte rushes to Eugene.)*

CHARLOTTE. Eugene! Are you alright? Did you swallow something? Hold on, let me get your water. *(She scurries into the kitchen. Eugene promptly ceases gagging, addresses Robert.)*

EUGENE. See what I did there?

ROBERT. Doing okay, boy?

EUGENE. Notice how she hastened to my side? Scurried off to fetch me water and other such sundries? Don't expect similar niceties to be delivered your way, sir.

ROBERT. She'll be right back, buddy.

EUGENE. Just because you're all macho and manly and such ... Hey! Don't "buddy" me. We are not comrades.

ROBERT. Oh, Eugene. This night is already not going the way I planned. *(He reveals a ring box from his pocket.)*

EUGENE. Cardigans and cardamom, sir, put that away! *(He swats the box out of Robert's hands.)*

ROBERT. Eugene! What was that about? *(He goes to fetch the box; Eugene trails him.)*

EUGENE. You, sir, have reached my capacity for composure. I can tolerate your plebeian presence no more! You can't just come traipsing into our lives with your boyish charm and your burly ways and your ... propensity for pepperoni!

ROBERT. Woah, shhh, buddy.

EUGENE. Ack! Mediocre alliterative insults are all I have left? *(Anguished.)* You have maimed me, Bobbert.

ROBERT. Sorry if I upset ya, fella. *(Charlotte returns with bowl of water; puts it on the toy box. Robert returns the ring box to his pocket. *PRODUCTION NOTE: This is the spot where the typical audience member has had their "Ah-ha" moment of realization: Eugene is a dog!)*

CHARLOTTE. Here you go, Eugene, drink up. Feel better. *(She moves to Robert's side. Eugene scampers to his water dish, sits, dips a finger, tastes.)*

EUGENE. Satisfactory, thank you.

ROBERT. Charlotte. I'm not sure he likes me.

CHARLOTTE. Eugene? Eugene likes everybody. Don'tcha buddy? *(Eugene stares at her blankly.)* Eugene loves you! We both love you. And I'm sure we're both going to love Bella.

ROBERT. Oh my God, Bella! She's probably torn the car apart by now. I should get her. Should I go get her? I'm gonna go get her. Is it time?

EUGENE. For your medication? Yes, here's some water.

CHARLOTTE. Yes, go get her. We'll be right here.

ROBERT. Okay, I'll take her for a little walk, let her do her thing. I'll be back, don't you worry! Hey, come here. I have this awesome, wonderful sense of hope for us.

CHARLOTTE. You have no idea how amazing that is to hear right now.

EUGENE. You're lucky I'm all gagged out.

ROBERT. Okay, be back in a minute. All right, Eugene? Okay, buddy? *(Eugene flings water in Robert's direction, undeterred.)* Hey, Eugene, I've brought you a new friend.

EUGENE. I can barely keep my sweater on. *(Robert exits. Eugene pulls at his sweater.)* No, really. Take this thing off.

CHARLOTTE. He really is quite wonderful, Eugene. Maybe there's nothing to worry about.

EUGENE. Jiminy Cricket, enough about that foolish creature. Let's focus on me. I'm itchy, I'm hot, I'm thirsty, I'm attention-starved and I'm cranky.

CHARLOTTE. Come here, big fella. What's wrong?

EUGENE. Was that not a comprehensive enough list?

CHARLOTTE. Tell me what's on your mind.

EUGENE. Well, since you ask, Charlotte, lately I've had this prevailing sense of ennui. And the argyle isn't helping. *(He pulls at his sweater.)*

CHARLOTTE. *(Fixing Eugene's sweater.)* Have I told you lately how handsome you look?

EUGENE. Yes, thank you, and I appreciate that. But, you see, so much of the purpose has drained from my life. When you're at the office, there's only so much to do. I entertain myself with Sudoku and the occasional crossword puzzle but unfortunately my knowledge of pop culture is decidedly limited.

CHARLOTTE. Eugene, can I tell you something?

EUGENE. You can tell me anything, always.

CHARLOTTE. There's gonna be some pretty big changes around here.

EUGENE. I'm not a strong proponent of change.

CHARLOTTE. And I know you're not a big fan of change, but I really think this could be good, for all of us.

EUGENE. All of us?

CHARLOTTE. Maybe I'm just afraid it's too good to be true, you know? Like I'm waiting for the other shoe to drop.

EUGENE. Mmm, shoes.

CHARLOTTE. I mean, I've been fooled by feelings before.

EUGENE. Foolish fickle feelings.

CHARLOTTE. But I'm not getting any younger.

EUGENE. Oh, you've got plenty of viable years left.

CHARLOTTE. *(Indicating her stomach.)* And everything just got really real.

EUGENE. Robert's an ignoramus if he doesn't realize what he has with you. That said, you are welcome to personally end it at any time. For example, you may end it now.

CHARLOTTE. Time just goes by so fast.

EUGENE. Or you can wait until he gets back, so he's aware of the finality of the ending.

CHARLOTTE. Eugene, do you remember the day you came to live here?

EUGENE. Charlotte, that was the best day of my life.

CHARLOTTE. You had that cute little argyle bowtie and you looked up at me with those bulbous, wondrous eyes. I had no idea what to do with you. Honestly! Not a clue. They just handed you over - here you go, you have a dog now. Take care of this creature. He's yours.

EUGENE. You placed me outside, and the sky was a certain shade of cerulean ... honestly, I saw more colors that day than I am genetically capable of perceiving. That's what you do to a fella.

CHARLOTTE. You had been there too long, Eugene.

EUGENE. I was waiting for you.

CHARLOTTE. I should've found you sooner.

EUGENE. You found me as soon as you could.

CHARLOTTE. And now look at you! You'll be dead before I know it.

EUGENE. What the Charles Dickens! Are such levels of morbidity necessary, Charlotte? Okay, so I may or may not die somewhere in the near future, but that means you shack up with Mister Potato Head? Because he's human and will potentially live longer than me?

CHARLOTTE. But I don't need to be alone my whole life.

EUGENE. No, you don't! I'm right here. Focus on me.

CHARLOTTE. I need to stop pushing people away.

EUGENE. No, no - push! Shoo, all the people!

CHARLOTTE. I mean, who knows, this could be the beginning of everything.

EUGENE. Oh, this is an intolerable line of conversation. You're not even listening to me!

CHARLOTTE. I don't know. Do you think it's too soon?

EUGENE. Well, it's too soon for me to die, but you seem to have that all mapped out.

CHARLOTTE. Eugene, come here. Gimme a hug. *(Eugene perks up; they approach one another, a knock at the door; Charlotte abandons the hug.)* Oh gosh, they're here! You ready to meet your new friend?

EUGENE. I don't think you grasp the irrelevance of my interest in this whole scene you and what's-his-face are contriving. *(Knocks on the door.)*

ROBERT. *(Offstage.)* Hey, Charlotte!

CHARLOTTE. Eugene, come here. *(Eugene moves away, gesturing wildly.)*

EUGENE. It's a dog! Meeting a dog. And you're making an entire production out of it!

ROBERT. *(Offstage.)* We good to come in?

EUGENE. Go away!

CHARLOTTE. Eugene, come here and be quiet. One second, Robert! *(To Eugene, who has retreated to corner.)* What is wrong with you? *(She opens the door; Robert enters.)*

ROBERT. Hey, hey, everyone!

CHARLOTTE. *(Awkward pause.)* Where is she?

ROBERT. Oh! She's in the hallway. C'mon Bella, let's meet Charlotte.

CHARLOTTE. Was she okay in the car?

ROBERT. Oh yeah, totally fine. C'mere, Bells. Bella! She must be feeling shy.

BELLA. *(From hallway.)* Ha!

ROBERT. Yes! Good girl. Come here.

CHARLOTTE. Come here, Bella!

BELLA. *(Hysterically from hallway.)* No, you come here! I don't want to go there! I think you should come here!

EUGENE. Oh good, that's what we need. Histrionics.

ROBERT. Bella ... *(Bella enters, looking adorable and decidedly grumpy.)*

CHARLOTTE. Aw, hey Bella! Look how cute you are!

BELLA. *(Warming up.)* Awww, yeah. That's true.

ROBERT. Come inside, Bella. This is Charlotte. *(Bella moves very close to Charlotte.)*

BELLA. Oh, helloooooooo.

CHARLOTTE. Oh, Robert, she's adorable.

ROBERT. Yup, she's my little fluff 'n stuff. *(Musses Bella's hair.)*

BELLA. I am! He loves me so much and I love him so much, and we just love each other!

CHARLOTTE. Well, it's nice to finally meet you, Bella.

BELLA. Right? He talks about you constantly. *(To Robert.)* You talk about her constantly. *(To Charlotte.)* I've never even met you and I'm already kinda sick of your face.

CHARLOTTE. Oh, she's lovely.

BELLA. You smell nice. I like snacks. *(To Robert.)* She's not as pretty as you said she'd be.

EUGENE. *(Has heard enough.)* Hogwash and fiddlesticks!

BELLA. Oh my goodness, hello! I didn't see you there!

EUGENE. She is the prettiest human person in the world! Now get out of my house, you foolish, uninformed creature!

BELLA. *(Yells.)* Oh my goodness why are you yelling at me? I don't even know you!

CHARLOTTE. Look, Robert - they're saying hi to each other.

ROBERT. She seems a little anxious, actually.

BELLA. What is wrong with you, Mister?

EUGENE. I'm perturbed you would malign Charlotte's

quite apparent pulchritude.

BELLA. Huh? *(Spots plant, runs to it.)* Oh my gosh! Alfred! What are you doing here?

EUGENE. Apologize to Charlotte immediately.

BELLA. *(To Alfred.)* Are you feeling okay? I missed you so much! I was thinking about the conversation we were having in the car, and you were right - we're together again!

CHARLOTTE. So what do you think, Eugene?

EUGENE. This is with whom you expect me to align myself?

BELLA. I don't think I like you, mister uppity pants.

EUGENE. Do you think I care what you think, miss "fluff 'n stuff"?

BELLA. Hey! Don't talk to me that way! *(To Robert.)* Don't let him talk to me that way! *(To Eugene.)* Why are you talking to me? Who are you, anyway?

EUGENE. Isn't it obvious? I'm your new friend.

BELLA. *(Let's it sink in.)* Oh ... my ... gosh!

EUGENE. I know.

BELLA. This is ... this is just wonderful! Alfred, did you hear that? *(Dances around, sings:)* Best day! This is the best day! Best day! This is the best day!

ROBERT. Aw, look. They're friends.

EUGENE. Oh, no, no, no - we are not friends. This, this is a misunderstanding.

BELLA. We are like the two best friends that ever, ever existed! *(She enthusiastically embraces Eugene, who shrieks.)*

EUGENE. Ah! Why is she touching me!? Extract her from my circumference of solitude!

BELLA. Oh, Eugene. I've always wanted a friend.

EUGENE. I have personally never experienced such insipid inclinations.

BELLA. Don't you think this is the bestest, most wonderfullest thing that's ever happened to us?

EUGENE. Decidedly not. Now please return to your owner. Over there. Shoo.

BELLA. But ... but Eugene!

EUGENE. Go. Shoo. Now. Shoo!

BELLA. *(Begrudgingly returns to Robert's side.)* Eugene doesn't like me. I like him and I think he's the swellest fella that ever existed but he doesn't like me, Bobby! Why doesn't he like me? And why is it so cold in here?

ROBERT. Hey, Bella. How ya doin' honey?

BELLA. I'm cold and I've been rejected! Hey! *(Points at Eugene.)* Why does he have a sweater and I don't have a sweater?

EUGENE. Please do not point at me. And please do not covet this sweater.

BELLA. But you look like the handsomest, warmest fella in the world!

EUGENE. I look like a serial killer.

BELLA. *(Shivers; gives moon-eyes to Robert.)* I'm so cold, Bobby.

ROBERT. Aw, Bella, what's up? She seem chilly to you?

BELLA. *(Jumps around, overjoyed.)* Yes! Exactly! Oh my gosh I love you! You know me inside and out and understand all my wants and needs!

ROBERT. No, I guess she's fine.

BELLA. *(Stops jumping around, resumes shivering; reprimands.)* No! Bobby! Bobby, I'm cold! Cover me in cotton and unabated adoration.

EUGENE. Unabated?

BELLA. Um, yeah, Eugene - unabated! I'm smart and know things, too! So Bobby, yeah? Pretty please?

ROBERT. I'm gonna run out to the car and grab her sweater.

CHARLOTTE. Okay, I'll wait here and watch them interact.

ROBERT. Let me know how it goes. *(He exits.)*

EUGENE. Interact? What is this? Are we in a glass enclosure? Are there levers to press in order to earn a treat? Am I a damn panda bear? I will not be denigrated in this way!

BELLA. I love pandas. *(Robert is gone.)* Bobby. Bobby, where did you go? *(Runs around, stricken, falls to floor.)* He's gone! It's over! My life is over.

CHARLOTTE. Hey, hey, darlin'. You're okay. He'll be right back.

BELLA. This is terrible. This is the worst day of my life. I'm gonna die. *(Notices Charlotte.)* Hi. You're pretty, and smell like sunshine. Are you my new family? Do you love me like a lot, lot, lot? Here, you may rub my ears. *(Charlotte obliges.)* This is the happiest I've ever been in my entire life.

EUGENE. Hey. Sociopath. Stay away from my person.

BELLA. Isn't she wonderful?

EUGENE. Well aware. Now step off.

BELLA. But Bobby left me!

EUGENE. And if you could hear over the sound of your own grousing, you would know he will return momentarily.

BELLA. *(Jumps up.)* Is it true? Bobby's coming back? Come back to me, Bobby!

EUGENE. Charlotte, I implore you: please end this charade. We still have ample time to prepare a delicious repast and settle down for Wheel of Fortune.

CHARLOTTE. Isn't she adorable, Eugene? I'm honestly a little surprised she's Robert's. I mean, I guess I imagined something a little more ...

EUGENE. Substantial?

CHARLOTTE. But she's so cute! And seeing them together - it's like seeing this different side of him. It makes me think, I don't know, you know?

EUGENE. I have no idea what anybody's talking about anymore. *(Robert knocks, enters with sweater.)*

ROBERT. Okay, got it.

BELLA. Bobby!

ROBERT. Bella ... Look what I got for ya ... *(He shows Bella the sweater; she runs in circles.)*

BELLA. A sweater! It's a sweater! It's a beautiful, magical sweater!

EUGENE. Oh, this is horrifying.

BELLA. Shut up, Eugene! Eugene, look at my sweater. Bobby brought me a sweater. Oh, dress me, Bobby! *(She holds out her arms in whimsical surrender. Robert dresses her.)*

EUGENE. You're an embarrassment to the canine community. And yourself.

BELLA. Don't be silly, Eugene; you're wearing a sweater, too!

EUGENE. Yes, against my will, Bella - against my will. You don't see me stretching my arms out in whimsical surrender.

BELLA. *(Runs to Eugene.)* Okay! Look! How do I look?

EUGENE. Let me see. You have an oddly shaped face,

and your expressions are sort of ... vapid. You're all bubbly and happy and vapid.

BELLA. *(Unaffected.)* No, silly! The sweater - how does the sweater look?

EUGENE. Solid colors would complement you better. Fewer patterns. You're discombobulated enough as it is.

BELLA. Ach! Why did I even come over here?

EUGENE. Valid point - you were far more attractive from across the room. Could you please take about 200 steps back?

BELLA. Oh, you ... *(She attacks Eugene; Charlotte and Robert rush over. Robert extracts Bella from the fray.)*

ROBERT. Bella! What are you doing? Get over here!

CHARLOTTE. Oh my God, Eugene! Are you okay?

EUGENE. Hold me, Charlotte. I'm scared. She's so scary.

BELLA. *(Staccato, like a bark.)* Shut up! Shut up! Shut up!

ROBERT. Bella, be quiet! What's gotten into you? I'm so sorry, Charlotte; she's never like this.

CHARLOTTE. They're just feeling each other out. I'm sure it's to be expected. *(To Eugene.)* Isn't it, darling? It's okay.

EUGENE. It is certainly not okay, Charlotte. You've turned our apartment into a side show circus act. I'm missing my soaps, I feel a touch of angina, and today's Sudoku certainly isn't going to sort itself out!

CHARLOTTE. There, there, darlin'. Shhh ...

EUGENE. Don't shush me. I shall not be shushed!

CHARLOTTE. *(Pulls Eugene close, shushing him.)* Calm down, Eugene. I've got you. Shhh ...

EUGENE. Okay ... *(He rests against Charlotte, effectively shushed.)*

BELLA. Your life sounds super boring.

EUGENE. Please stay over there.

BELLA. Is that really all you do with your day?

EUGENE. You are possibly the worst thing that's ever happened to me.

BELLA. Um, whoa, this has been a hard day for me, too, Eugie. I was stuck in that car for like... three days! Plus! You called me ugly.

EUGENE. False, I called you more attractive from far away. For example, right now - you look lovely.

BELLA. Oh, why thank you, Eugene.

EUGENE. In your oh-so-stylish sweater.

BELLA. Fine! You don't want me to wear the sweater? I won't wear the sweater! I hate this sweater! I hate it, I hate it! *(She struggles out of her sweater; shoves it in her mouth.)*

EUGENE. So now you're going to eat the sweater.

ROBERT. Bella! What are you doing? C'mon, give me that. *(He takes the sweater from Bella, who snatches it back with her hand; they begin a tug of war.)* Give it.

BELLA. No.

ROBERT. Bella, let go.

BELLA. Bobby, don't take away my sweater! I love this sweater!

ROBERT. Bella dog. Do you wanna go back to the car?

BELLA. Look, Eugene, he's playing with me.

EUGENE. He's not playing with you. He's trying to salvage the sweater for which he probably paid far too much money.

BELLA. *(Confronts Eugene, throwing Robert back.)* Listen to me, buster.

ROBERT. Bella!

CHARLOTTE. Wait, Robert, they're trying to be friends again.

BELLA. No, I'm coming over here to tell your dog he's a big-headed, smelly-faced bully.

EUGENE. Well, you just ruined a perfectly nice sweater.

BELLA. What is your problem, mister?

EUGENE. Oh, okay, let's see - you come in here, disrupt my deliciously serene lifestyle, insult my person, and I'm the one with the problem?

BELLA. Ugh! I'm sorry about what I said, okay? She's very pretty. *(To Charlotte.)* You're so, so, so pretty. *(To Eugene.)* Better?

EUGENE. Moderately.

BELLA. And your lifestyle is not serene; it's boring. And if our people want us to be friends and they know us better than any other peoples in the whole world then maybe it's because we should be friends! Maybe even like best friends - Oh! Yes! Let's choose that one! Best friends!

EUGENE. Would you like my honest reaction to this proposal?

BELLA. Absolutely! *(Eugene pretends to hack up all over the floor. Charlotte rushes over to pat his back.)*

CHARLOTTE. There, there, darlin'.

EUGENE. *(Straightens up, realizes.)* Actually, I do feel a bit bilious. Perhaps it's time for our evening tea. Charlotte?

CHARLOTTE. All better. *(Returns to Robert's side.)* Eugene is acting very strange today. Perhaps I should socialize him more.

EUGENE. Oh, dear God, no. Please, please, no.

BELLA. Hack up all you want, Eugene, but I know we

should be friends - we should be best, best friends!

EUGENE. You're a bit slow, aren't you? I'm trying my absolute best not to judge.

BELLA. Fine, I give up! You're stupid! *(To Charlotte.)* And you're pretty, okay? You're very pretty. *(To Robert.)* And you! You've thrown me to the wolves! And taken my sweater! I'm so cold; I loved that sweater, Bobby. I trusted you! We should be snuggling. We should be happy! This is not a happy place! I'm going now. I'm gonna sit by this door and I'm gonna kick it and scratch it until you take me home. *(She flops by the front door, kicks it.)*

EUGENE. Oh, wow.

CHARLOTTE. Do you think she's all right?

ROBERT. She's fine. She'll get over it.

BELLA. I will not get over it!

EUGENE. *(Grabs his Sudoku and sits.)* I'm over it.

CHARLOTTE. *(Mildly defeated, sits on couch.)* Oh, this isn't going as well as we hoped, huh?

ROBERT. *(Joins Charlotte.)* Well. Dogs are weird. *(A moment, then: Loud knocks at the front door.)*

SUZANNE. *(Offstage)* Yoo-hoo!

BELLA. What is that?!

ROBERT. Who could that be?

CHARLOTTE. It must be Suzanne. You know, my neighbor, the one I told you about.

ROBERT. Oh, the um ... *(Clears throat.)*

CHARLOTTE. The, um, what?

ROBERT. The um ... the very nice lady who lives across the hall?

CHARLOTTE. Robert, I don't know what you're trying not to say, but "nice" isn't the first descriptor I would use for Suzie.

SUZANNE. *(Shouts offstage.)* Hey, Charlotte, my little starlet! It's Suzie! Let me in!

EUGENE. Oh, heaven help us.

SUZANNE. *(Offstage.)* Yoo-hoo! *(She pushes against the door.)*

BELLA. *(Freaking out.)* What's happening? What is this?

CHARLOTTE. Come in, Suzanne!

SUZANNE. *(Offstage.)* Well, what do you think it is I'm trying to do?

ROBERT. Come here, Bella. Out of the doorway.

BELLA. No, no, no, no, no!

CHARLOTTE. Come here, darlin', let Suzie in.

SUZANNE. *(Offstage.)* Charlotte!

EUGENE. *(Moves to assist.)* Oh, good heavens, let's just move this hysterical creature to another room and calm everyone down -

CHARLOTTE. Eugene, calm down, get out of the way, please. Thank you.

BELLA. Yeah, go away, Eugene! You're ignorant and stupid!

EUGENE. Yes, clearly I am the problem here. *(He goes to sit far away.)*

CHARLOTTE. Good boy, Eugene.

EUGENE. Yes, I'll return to my corner. To my now tepid water that does little to truly nourish me.

SUZANNE. *(Offstage.)* Charlotte, what is going on in there?

BELLA. Take me home or I will throw up all over this rug!

CHARLOTTE. One minute, Suzanne! Hold on. *(To

Robert.) Should we just put her in the bathroom for a minute?

ROBERT. Great idea. Come here, Bella. *(He drags Bella into the hallway.)*

SUZANNE. *(Offstage.)* So far, Charlotte, this has been a highly un-enjoyable visit.

EUGENE. Really? I find this lovely. *(Suzanne enters; loud, abrasive, a bit tipsy. She wears a vivacious dance costume.)*

SUZANNE. Good Lord, people. Pull yourselves together. Here I take a night off, thinking maybe, you know, I should finally meet this man you've been puking up sparkles about and what do you do? You barricade the door with barking bohemian beasties.

CHARLOTTE. Suzanne, I'm so sorry, I should've warned you. The dogs just met and it's been a little crazy as they -

SUZANNE. Okay, pause. Pause it all right there. Your dogs just met?

CHARLOTTE. Yes.

SUZANNE. As in, they had a meeting.

CHARLOTTE. Yes.

SUZANNE. As in a pre-arranged, specially planned meeting just for your dogs?

EUGENE. Clarify it as many times as you'd like.

CHARLOTTE. Yes, Suzanne. They wanted to meet.

EUGENE. I was pretty clear about that not being the case. *(Robert returns; Charlotte takes his arm.)*

CHARLOTTE. We wanted them to meet so we planned for them to meet.

SUZANNE. Lordy, well, there's your issue. Ah, no, your primary issue was becoming a dog owner in the first place. Your secondary issue was dating another dog owner ...

regardless of how attractive. Hello, I'm Suzanne.

ROBERT. Um, hi, it's nice to meet -

SUZANNE. Don't bother with formalities. I have very little patience for anyone willing to sacrifice their own personal needs for the whims of a whiny canine. I respect that everyone has their deep-seated Freudian issues or whatnot, but it's messed up.

CHARLOTTE. Suzanne!

SUZANNE. It's messed up! I'm sorry, but it's true! They urinate on your hardwood floors and you consider it the Mona Lisa.

ROBERT. I really don't think my dog's urine is a work of art-

SUZANNE. Plus, I just can't get behind the whole idea of sleeping with the same creature that just rubbed its fecal matter across the living room carpet.

ROBERT. ... I can appreciate that.

EUGENE. Excuse me?

SUZANNE. Am I gonna get a name?

EUGENE. Slanderer!

CHARLOTTE. Eugene, shush.

SUZANNE. Do we have a name?

ROBERT. Name? Oh, sorry. Her name is Bella.

SUZANNE. *(Pause.)* See? This is what I am talking about - this, this is why I'm worried about you, Charlotte.

CHARLOTTE. Honey, I think she meant your name. Suzanne, this is Robert. Robert, this is my neighbor, Suzanne.

SUZANNE. Nice to meet you, Robert. Unless you prefer I call you Bella?

EUGENE. He might.

ROBERT. Robert is fine.

SUZANNE. Wait, how have we not met? How have I not met this guy? Have you been hiding him away? *(Appreciatively.)* Mm, Mm, Mm.

CHARLOTTE. Nothing of the sort, Suzanne. We're hardly ever here together except Fridays and that's when you have your rumba lessons.

SUZANNE. Samba. And yeah, I'm done with all that. It was good while it lasted, but Alejandro only had so much to offer and it just ... wasn't enough. If you know what I mean, Bobby.

ROBERT. Uh, no. I ... nope.

SUZANNE. So tell me something, Bobby -

CHARLOTTE. He prefers Robert.

SUZANNE. Well, Bella, here's the deal. Charlotte's like a daughter to me. I know I may seem abrasive, a bit rough around the edges, but ... well, it's true. I'll kill ya. I'll kill ya when you least expect it and I'll leave that ridiculous little pompadour to die alone in her crate.

ROBERT. I think you mean to say "Maltese", and I've actually never crated her -

SUZANNE. Yes, yes, I'm sure you prefer to sleep with her fecal matter all close to your face and snuggled up to ya. I get it, Freud gets it, we all get it. But Charlotte means the sun and the moon to me, and if you mess with her, you're messing with me. And I am really, really messy.

CHARLOTTE. *(Awkward silence.)* Okay, then. I'm sure you won't mind if I get back to prepping dinner -

SUZANNE. What? Oh, dear girl, no. No, no, no. Go fix your face or whatever you young chickies do. Then this perplexing yet strikingly good-looking man is going to take you out, out, away from this place, for a nice dinner.

ROBERT. Actually -

SUZANNE. What's the matter, Bobby? Can't afford a nice dinner? Is it too much to ask for you to take this incredible young woman out for a romantic dinner by candlelight without dog fur all up in y'all's face?

ROBERT. We actually go out all the time. don't we, honey? And Bella doesn't shed, in fact she's hypoallergenic -

SUZANNE. Yes, I know. Bella is the perfect woman. Yes. She's also a dog. But this, here, this is an actual woman. And you're going to wine and dine her and get her out of this apartment in which she spends far too much time. What d'you even do in here?

EUGENE. *(Stepping forward.)* Actually, we have an assortment of both board games and crossword puzzles that keep us fairly occupied-

SUZANNE. *(Retreating.)* Aaaaah! Why is that thing approaching me? What does it want?

CHARLOTTE. Oh, he's harmless. Suzanne, you know Eugene.

SUZANNE. Just because I see him every damn day doesn't mean we're on a first name basis. Shoo!

EUGENE. Charlotte is a complicated and classy woman with a rich and rewarding inner life. *(Pause.)* You seem to be insinuating otherwise and I wished to clarify. *(He returns to sit in his corner.)*

SUZANNE. Charlotte, your dog is very strange.

CHARLOTTE. It might be the sweater.

SUZANNE. Yeah, that's another thing, dressing them up like that.

ROBERT. Oh, Bella loves it. When I go to pick out her outfit, she runs right over and picks it out for herself. I think she likes how it keeps her comfy and warm and ... *(Spots Suzanne staring.)* Never mind.

SUZANNE. I'm gonna choose to overlook all of ... that. Why're we still standing here? Go! Get ready. He's taking you to dinner.

CHARLOTTE. *(To Robert.)* Is that all right?

SUZANNE. Of course it's all right. Go! And take that furry ... creature thing with you.

CHARLOTTE. Come on, Eugene.

EUGENE. *(To Suzanne, affronted.)* You, madam, insult me.

CHARLOTTE. And, Suzie, there's something I want to talk to you about. Something important.

SUZANNE. Oh sweetie, now you've got me all titillated. *(To Eugene.)* Shoo! Go, go with your mother thing. *(Charlotte and Eugene exit to the bedroom hallway.)* Such strange creatures ... with those big, bug eyes. Makes you wonder what they're thinking. Can't trust 'em. *(Long pause.)* You're a good lookin' fella.

ROBERT. Um. Thank you.

SUZANNE. I'm a little bit intoxicated.

ROBERT. Oh? I didn't even ... okay. That's ... that's okay.

SUZANNE. I love that girl, you know. That girl ... the one you're dating.

ROBERT. Charlotte's easy to love -

SUZANNE. Charlotte, yes! But lemme tell ya, that girl has dated some doozies. Some real cads. Jerks. Losers. Bums. None of 'em worth a second glance. None of 'em. But there she goes, lookin' again and again, seeing the best in people.

ROBERT. She's one of a kind, that's for sure. *(Bella comes to hallway door, listens.)*

SUZANNE. All I'm sayin', Bobby, is I hope you're not one of those guys. She can't take another one of those guys.

ROBERT. I ... I don't want to be one of those guys.

SUZANNE. Don't be.

ROBERT. I'm not! I'm not one of those guys. I just wanna be worthy of her.

SUZANNE. Well, you see, Bobby, it's not a matter of "want". You either are, or you aren't. And if you're not, skedaddle. Shoo. Leave us alone. And take your stupid fluffy thing with you.

BELLA. *(Leaps forward, circles Suzanne.)* Hey!

SUZANNE. Oh Lord, I summoned it! Get it away!

BELLA. This woman. I don't know about this woman, Bobby. Kinda wanna bite her.

ROBERT. Suzanne, this is my dog, Bella. She's harmless.

SUZANNE. Ah, yes. Your perfect female. Lemme see the little shit ... zu.

ROBERT. Maltese.

SUZANNE. Excuse me?

ROBERT. Never mind. Bella, say hi.

BELLA. No.

ROBERT. Bella.

BELLA. Hi.

SUZANNE. Yes. You. Hello, little fluff-face. *(She taps Bella twice on the head.)*

ROBERT. See? She's harmless. And pretty adorable.

SUZANNE. Eh, I'll stick to martinis.

BELLA. I'm so bored of meeting people, Bobby. Let's go home and snuggle.

SUZANNE. Speaking of martinis, I'm heading back

across the hall. Take care of my girl, Bobby, buy her a nice meal. Don't take her to some pizza joint.

ROBERT. Got it covered.

CHARLOTTE. *(Offstage.)* Eugene! What are you doing? Come back here! *(Eugene enters on a mission, bra atop head, straight to Suzanne. Charlotte follows, dressed for dinner. Eugene points a hairbrush at Suzanne, who lets out a shriek.)*

EUGENE. Sudoku is a stimulating, brain-enriching activity.

CHARLOTTE. Eugene! *(Suzanne presses up against the wall.)*

EUGENE. Charlotte also knits! She knits me sweaters. And socks. And pillows with my name on them. My name is "Eugene", and it looks lovely in a deep purple stitch. And she can accurately answer a small fraction of Jeopardy questions and you don't even know what you're talking about!

SUZANNE. What does it want from me, Charlotte - WHAT DOES IT WANT FROM ME?

CHARLOTTE. *(Retrieves her bra.)* I'm so sorry, Suzanne. It's been a hectic day -

EUGENE. I want you to take it back! We have a wonderful time in this apartment and Charlotte doesn't need anything else in order to be a complete woman.

CHARLOTTE. It's just all the craziness of meeting a new dog and everything that's been going on with Robert.

EUGENE. Don't go bringing Bobbert into this, Charlotte. This is between you and me and me and Suzanne here and Suzanne and you. Not him. And definitely not her.

BELLA. Eugene, you're freaking everybody out.

EUGENE. *(Calmly begins brushing Charlotte's hair.)* Shh,

you seem stressed. I think it's best if the ... other people leave. Let's curl up and read a good book.

CHARLOTTE. Eugene, I'm not sure what to say to you right now.

EUGENE. Say that you love me and we'll always be together.

CHARLOTTE. *(Grabs the hairbrush.)* Eugene, what are you - stop that, give me this! Go sit. Do you need a time out? Go sit. *(Eugene cowers, sits. Charlotte turns to everyone.)* I'm so sorry about that, everybody.

SUZANNE. Charlotte. I will never understand or support any of this. I'm leaving now.

CHARLOTTE. Wait, Suzie! A favor -

SUZANNE. Oh, here we go.

CHARLOTTE. It's not bad, not a big deal, it's just ... if Robert and I are going out, per your request -

SUZANNE. Because it's a fabulous idea.

CHARLOTTE. A fabulous idea, Suzie, thank you. But it means the pups will be home alone, and it being their first time together ...

SUZANNE. Just spit it out, Chiquita.

CHARLOTTE. They shouldn't be left unsupervised that whole time.

SUZANNE. For the length of an entrée.

CHARLOTTE. Could you please just check in on them? Poke your pretty little head in once or twice and make sure they're okay?

SUZANNE. Seriously?

CHARLOTTE. Pretty please?

BELLA. Cherry on top!

SUZANNE. Oh Dios mío. *(Oh my God).* You people.

Next time, I'm living in a place with a clear "No Pets" policy. *(She dramatically exits.)*

ROBERT. So ... was that a yes?

CHARLOTTE. That was a yes.

BELLA. Wait, wait wait. Bobby, is it true? You're gonna leave me here in this terrible place with that psychotic creature?

EUGENE. *(Stands.)* Oh, deal with your issues!

BELLA. Seriously, Eugene, did you just see yourself?

CHARLOTTE. Eugene, shush. Sit.

BELLA. Yeah, Eugene, shush. Sit.

ROBERT. Bella, come here. Give Eugene some space.

CHARLOTTE. Maybe we shouldn't go out. You know, just because Suzie has an idea doesn't mean we all need to jump -

ROBERT. It's a great idea; we just need to get them settled.

CHARLOTTE. Okay, I'm just gonna pop in the kitchen to clean things up. Sorry for the fuss, Robert. She grows on you, you know - Suzanne. She's been very good to me.

EUGENE. Ha!

CHARLOTTE. *(Warning.)* Eugene.

EUGENE. She is off her rocker.

CHARLOTTE. Eugene, come here. *(Eugene reluctantly shuffles over to Charlotte.)* Eugene, I don't know what's going on with you today, but I need you to behave. Bella needs a friend -

BELLA. I do. It's true.

CHARLOTTE. And I need to know I can leave you two alone.

BELLA. I need a best friend.

EUGENE. *(Snaps.)* I'm speaking with Charlotte!

CHARLOTTE. Eugene! This is exactly what I'm talking about!

EUGENE. Ah, I suppose it is. My apologies.

CHARLOTTE. Can I leave you two together?

BELLA. Ooh, yes! We will play games and chew on *(Grabs something.)* this and maybe even snuggle for a while as I sing him a lullaby ...

EUGENE. None of this will happen! But yes, enjoy your evening, Charlotte. I won't stand in your way.

CHARLOTTE. Good boy. *(Quieter, to Eugene.)* I'm uncomfortable with the thought of you being unhappy.

EUGENE. I'm uncomfortable with everything, but I will try to be better. *(Charlotte exits to kitchen. Bella dances around as Eugene skedaddles to his corner.)*

BELLA. *(Sings.)* Yay, we're gonna have a sleepover! We're gonna snuggle and share secrets! We're gonna play with Alfred and–

ROBERT. Bella! Bella, come here. Same goes for you; I need you to behave and be nice to Eugene here while Charlotte and I go out to dinner.

BELLA. Bobby. I love you.

ROBERT. You get me?

BELLA. Sometimes I love you so much I think I might just die.

ROBERT. Good girl.

BELLA. Like when you rub my tummy right here and go "shnookadoodle darlin-face" and give me lots of kisses ... sometimes I die a little bit, Bobby, inside my heart.

EUGENE. Oh, good Lord.

BELLA. From love.

EUGENE. This is highly disturbing.

BELLA. I die from love, Eugene! That's how much I could love you!

EUGENE. Please do not threaten me in my own home. *(Charlotte enters, looks at Bella and Eugene, who are momentarily quiet.)*

CHARLOTTE. Okay, well then, let's go!

ROBERT. Quick, before they rebel. *(Robert and Charlotte grab keys, purse; exit. Bella and Eugene are alone. Bella raises her arms in profound happiness; Eugene's eyes widen. Robert and Charlotte reenter.)* Okay, we should probably, I dunno, crate them? Tie them up? Medicate them?

CHARLOTTE. Separate them?

ROBERT. Great idea!

EUGENE. Excellent. I will grab my Sudoku and retire to my bedchamber.

CHARLOTTE. Let's put Bella in the bedroom. Eugene, stay here.

ROBERT. Perfect. C'mon, Bells.

BELLA. But I want to play with Eugene! *(She pouts but follows Robert out of the room. Eugene approaches Charlotte.)*

EUGENE. Are you sure you know what you're getting into?

CHARLOTTE. I have no idea what's going on anymore.

EUGENE. I'm serious, Charlotte- he looks at you like smooth Colombian coffee and he desperately needs a pick-me-up because he stayed up way too late watching football the night before. What I'm saying is, he's reaching - really high - and he, you know, makes you super happy and stuff and you'll probably share a wonderful life together but what about me!?

CHARLOTTE. Isn't Bella adorable?

EUGENE. No! This is exactly what I'm talking about: what about me? *(Robert returns.)*

ROBERT. All set.

CHARLOTTE. Thank you, dear.

ROBERT. Dear. I like that.

CHARLOTTE. Well, you are very dear to me. And seeing you with Bella ...

ROBERT. Oh my gosh, isn't she the cutest? *(Eugene flops on the couch, defeated.)*

CHARLOTTE. Yeah, like that. This side of you.

ROBERT. I know, not very manly ...

CHARLOTTE. It's the best kind of manly. I love this side of you.

ROBERT. Well, I should show it more often, then.

CHARLOTTE. You should.

ROBERT. I will. You're wonderful. May I escort you to dinner, m'lady?

CHARLOTTE. You may, kind sir. *(Robert exits; Charlotte goes to leave, pauses.)* See, Eugene? He's not so bad, right?

EUGENE. Well, I mean ... he certainly loves you.

CHARLOTTE. Take care of the house, Eugie.

EUGENE. Don't forget I love you, too. *(Charlotte blows Eugene a kiss; exits. Eugene catches the kiss; puts it in his pocket for later. Mutters to himself. Goes to his toy chest, takes out his robe and slippers and gets comfortable. He retrieves his Sudoku and reclines. Contentment. Then the sound of scrapes, a bang. A bit of pitter-patter and Bella bursts through the door.)*

BELLA. *(Singing.)* The sun will come out! Here I am! Through the forest and the trees and the tiny little bees - I found my way to you! *(Eugene chooses silence.)* They thought they could keep us apart, but they can never keep us apart! We love each other!

EUGENE. That we do not.

BELLA. We do, and it's wonderful. This time together is wonderful. I'm glad we met. There's something magical about toasters, and I believe world peace is possible in our lifetime. *(Eugene eyes Bella warily; she is very close.)* We should snuggle. *(Eugene escapes.)*

EUGENE. All right, that's it! You can't come in here looking all adorable and sprinkling sparkles everywhere and expect me to just take it! How did you get out of your room?

BELLA. I pushed open the door. But I would've chewed through the door, Eugene, to be here with you.

EUGENE. That's insane.

BELLA. And now here we are!

EUGENE. Go away! This is my house and you don't belong in it!

BELLA. But maybe I do, Eugene. Maybe now I belong here, too. *(Takes pillow off couch.)* Maybe these are my pillows, too. *(Eugene grabs pillow; proceeds to rip it apart.)*

EUGENE. No! Not your pillow! My pillow! *(Eugene tosses the pillow remains to the ground.)*

BELLA. Oh, Eugene! Now it's nobody's pillow!

EUGENE. But it's definitely not yours.

BELLA. Eugene, you're messing up our pretty little house.

EUGENE. My pretty little house! Charlotte's pretty little

house! You don't get to be here. You don't get to sit on my couch and play with my toys and look at my ... *(Grabs a slipper off his foot, throws it.)* slippers!

BELLA. Ew! Keep your smelly feet to yourself!

EUGENE. Keep your smelly face to yourself!

BELLA. My face smells like chicken and sweet potato in a delightful gravy sauce! *(Eugene opens his toy-box; throws dog toys and paraphernalia at Bella, who is excited to play.)*

EUGENE. I smite thee!

BELLA. I love thee!

EUGENE. I will not tolerate these shenanigans!

BELLA. She-nanny-nanny! This is fun, Eugene!

EUGENE. Out!

BELLA. Ooh, I have this one, Eugene! *(Suzanne enters with a martini glass, wearing a kimono.)*

SUZANNE. Ah! Holy rollers of Minnesota, what is going on in here?

EUGENE. So, you have returned!

BELLA. You're so pretty!

SUZANNE. Good Lord, I already suck at my job.

BELLA. Join the party, Suzie!

EUGENE. This is not a party! And this is not your house, nor yours! It is nobody's house but mine!

SUZANNE. This is why no one should trust me to take care of anything.

BELLA. And Charlotte, Eugie. It's Charlotte's house, too!

EUGENE. Don't throw facts at me, you little fluff-face! Get out, get out, get out!

SUZANNE. *(Spots apron; dons it, prepares to clean.)* Hey, cute little doggies! Let's just clean all this up and settle down, ya pooper-scoopers.

EUGENE. You settle down!

BELLA. *(Sings.)* Let's settle down together! Raise a family on a farm!

EUGENE. Out! Out! Out!

BELLA. With lots of little piglets and other animals of a cute nature!

SUZANNE. Good doggies. Nice doggies. *(She feels something in the apron pocket; extracts the pregnancy stick.)* Oh, good golly miss Molly.

BELLA. *(Grabs the stick from Suzanne.)* Ooh, what's this?

SUZANNE. Hey! Give that back!

BELLA. Look, Eugene, a new toy! We can chew on it.

EUGENE. We will never simultaneously chew on anything.

SUZANNE. *(Picks up a dog toy and squeaks it.)* Hey, little doggies. Let's all focus on something else. *(Grabs the stick and puts it in the plant.)* There, all gone.

BELLA. Oh, look! Alfred's gonna play with us, too!

EUGENE. Madame, what have you done to compromise my newly acquired shrubbery? *(Sniffs Alfred.)* Huh, Charlotte has already claimed my tree.

SUZANNE. *(Sits; this has taken a lot out of her.)* Well, the good news is now she won't trust me to babysit.

EUGENE. Suzanne, what is this item in my tree?!

BELLA. It's all of ours, Eugie! *(Jumps on couch; surveys land)* Now we share everything!

SUZANNE. Everyone just, shh. This is a safe space.

EUGENE. Oh yeah? We share everything, like one big dim-witted family? Well, I say hogwash and horticulture to that!

SUZANNE. Let's all just gather 'round, pour ourselves a drink, and hash this out like reasonable people.

BELLA. *(Joins Suzanne.)* Suzie, I think that's a great idea.

EUGENE. You wanna know how mine all this is? Well, I'll show you, I'll teach you the borderlines of my territory! *(He unzips fly; prepares to "claim" the plant.)*

SUZANNE. *(Together.)* Eugene, no!

BELLA. *(Together.)* Eugene, no!

    Blackout.

END OF ACT I

<u>ACT TWO</u>

Eugene is squished between Suzanne and Bella on the couch: they have been there a while.

Suzanne, drink in hand, expounds:

SUZANNE. Tell me, furry little creatures. Do you ever think about metamorphosis?

EUGENE. Not particularly a Kafka fan.

SUZANNE. You know … metamorphosis. Changing. Becoming something different, something better.

EUGENE. I wasn't aware I could actually be improved.

SUZANNE. A more accurate representation of yourself, a better version.

EUGENE. I hear you. I am simply unable to relate.

SUZANNE. Sometimes, my skin just feels wrong, you know?

EUGENE. That's concerning, actually. You should look into that.

SUZANNE. I'm a delicate flower, you know. I feel things quite intensely. Alejandro never really got that, never really understood me. I think I scared him. Maybe if my outsides were delicate like my insides ... I don't know, maybe he could ... Maybe it would be easier to love me.

BELLA. Ooh, ooh, I understand! Like how I'm cute and adorable and everybody loves me!

EUGENE. Your sense of empathy is sadly misaligned.

SUZANNE. I'm a delicate flower!

BELLA. You are!

EUGENE. Au contraire, Suzanne; delicate flower you are not.

BELLA. Eugene, you're not helping!

EUGENE. No, perpetuating misconceptions regarding Suzanne's sense of self is not helping. This will only lead to continued confusion and repeated capitulation into her cups followed by subsequent feelings of despair.

BELLA. Oh, that sounds terrible. Suzie, I think you're a beautiful flower.

EUGENE. I give up.

SUZANNE. *(Defeated.)* I'm a potato.

EUGENE. Ah, now we have a more appropriate appellation!

BELLA. No! Eugene!

EUGENE. Let's at least start from a more reasonable postulate. Suzanne, let's say you are a potato.

SUZANNE. I am a potato!

BELLA. Suzanne, you are not a potato.

EUGENE. I said she's a damn potato!

SUZANNE. I am a potato!

EUGENE. All right, capital, yes - but! Suzanne, let us specify - what kind of potato are you?

SUZANNE. But ... I am a sweet potato!

BELLA. A very sweet potato!

EUGENE. A moderately saccharine sweet potato.

SUZANNE. With freshly churned butter.

BELLA. And brown sugar!

SUZANNE. And a scoop of brown sugar slathered on top.

All mixed together y delicioso.

EUGENE. Okay, well, we just lost most of the nutritional value of said potato, but simultaneously gained an important insight. Suzanne, yes, you may be a potato. But! You are an exceptional one.

BELLA. Eugene, that was very kind.

SUZANNE. I feel like you two really understand.

BELLA. Oh, we do!

EUGENE. I do.

SUZANNE. I never really gave you guys a chance, but I get it now: you guys are great, just really great. Bella, right? *(Bella nods vigorously, yes.)* Bella, do you know how to samba? *(Shakes vigorously, no.)* Wanna learn how? *(Bella nods vigorously, yes. Suzanne squeals, reaches for Bella.)* Right now, Alejandro would be holding me in his arms, like this. *(Initially alarmed, Bella relaxes.)*

BELLA. Oh. Okay, this is nice.

SUZANNE. He would be counting the steps, teaching me the turns. I never listened to a thing he said, you know; I know absolutely nothing about the samba.

EUGENE. Yes, we can see that.

SUZANNE. It wasn't what he said; it was the way he said it. That intoxicating voice of his laced with pineapples and jalapeños. Alejandro knew how to shake awake my soul, he treated me like I mattered; looked at me like a flower delicada *(Delicate).*

EUGENE. A potato flower.

BELLA. Shush, Eugene! Yes, Suzanne, I feel it. My heart seems bigger when we dance like this.

SUZANNE. Alejandro, oh, mi Alejandro! How you make me feel like a delicate flower!

BELLA. Eugene, you should try!

EUGENE. I don't much care to feel like una flor delicada, gracias.

BELLA. No, silly, the dancing! *(Pulls at Eugene.)* C'mon!

EUGENE. Let me alone. *(He breaks away; catches Suzanne's eye.)*

SUZANNE. Oh! Eugene, sweetie. Would you care to cut in?

EUGENE. Certainly not.

SUZANNE. Come here, big guy, your turn. Dance me to the moon!

EUGENE. *(Approaches in order to correct.)* It's fly me to the moon, actually.

BELLA. Yay, Eugene! Fly to the moon!

EUGENE. No, no "yay Eugene" -

SUZANNE. *(Grabs Eugene for a dance.)* Ya old kook, join the party.

EUGENE. I must insist, this will not do -

SUZANNE. You are a magnificent creature, Eugene. *(Resistance is futile.)*

EUGENE. Yes, well, that much is true-

SUZANNE. Ah, Eugene mi querido! Lo siento. *(My dear one! I'm sorry.)* I'm sorry I spent the last few years thinking you were a smelly old beast. I was judging you.

EUGENE. You were.

SUZANNE. I was, and I'm sorry for that. But now! Now I see what a delightful and sensitive creature you are! You, my little snickerdoodle, are a wonderful bundle of fluff! *(Suzanne hugs Eugene, so Bella hugs Eugene, too.)*

BELLA. He is! He is! My bundle of fluff! *(All are intertwined in a group hug.)*

SUZANNE. *(Crying/laughing.)* I am so happy!

BELLA. I need air.

EUGENE. I need a nap.

SUZANNE. *(Releases everybody.)* I need a drink!

EUGENE. Excellent, let's all just go our merry ways -

SUZANNE. Oh, you marvelous little man, you! *(She grabs Eugene; gives him a big smooch.)*

EUGENE. Ah! I am a prisoner in my own home!

SUZANNE. *(Saunters to the bar; pours a fresh glass.)* Well, what a delightful evening we're all having ... *(She raises the glass; Eugene snatches it.)*

EUGENE. Nothing is sacred. *(Swallows contents, returns glass, and retreats to corner.)* I abdicate responsibility for all of you.

SUZANNE. *(Unperturbed, pours another glass.)* Dance me to the moon! Ah, mi Alejandro. I drink, but it does not erase your memory, mi corazón. ¿Estás pensando en mí ahora? *(My heart. Are you thinking of me now?)* Do you sense my lack of presence by your side? Am I swimming through your senses as you samba your way into the night?

BELLA. Oh, you miss Alejandro very much.

SUZANNE. Bella, Bella beautiful, ven aquí. *(Come here.)* You wanna drink? Here's a drink. Drink responsibly. *(Bella sniffs the drink.)*

EUGENE. No! Bella does not need a drink! She is high on the catnip of life! *(Snatches glass; swallows contents.)* It's a disgrace.

BELLA. Aw, thanks Eugene.

EUGENE. Shut up. *(He pours another, finishing bottle; returns to his corner to nurse his drink.)*

BELLA. Eugene loves me.

SUZANNE. You two are adorable, you know. Just adorable. Why did I never get a dog? Oh, yeah. Can't stand 'em. *(Discovers empty bottle.)* Oh, lookie here, all gone. There's gotta be more of this somewhere. Hold on to ya horse an' buggies ya little bark faces, I'll be right back. *(She dramatically exits to kitchen. Eugene inspects his glass; Bella skips to his side.)*

EUGENE. I'm not sure this substance was designed for hydration.

BELLA. Eugene, I love you! I love you, I do!

EUGENE. Did you drink some of this, too?

BELLA. No. It's just the way I feel inside.

EUGENE. I feel funny.

BELLA. That's 'cuz you're a super funny guy, Eugene! *(A loud crash from the kitchen.)*

SUZANNE. *(Offstage.)* I'm totally fine!

EUGENE. I am not funny. And everyone tends to dislike me.

BELLA. That's not true, Eugene!

EUGENE. Well, it is.

BELLA. It's not!

EUGENE. It is.

BELLA. But I love you!

EUGENE. See, you keep saying that, and I feel like it sets up a certain expectation from me, from me to you. Something I simply cannot give.

BELLA. All I want is to be best friends forever and ever.

EUGENE. That's a long time-

BELLA. And ever.

EUGENE. Yes, well, that's an awfully long time.

BELLA. Or maybe just until you die.

EUGENE. *(Raises his glass.)* Which, according to popular opinion, will not be very long!

BELLA. Yay! Best friends until you die! I know you don't like me very much, Eugene, and that's okay. 'Cuz I'm pretty sure you don't like nobody very much.

EUGENE. Anybody. And with the exception of Charlotte, you are correct. I find other creatures excessively tiresome, especially the canine variety. *(Bella pouts. Eugene experiences remorse.)* But, hey there, you know ... my father once told me, before I was callously tossed into a cage - he said: "Exceptio probat regulam in casibus non exceptis."

BELLA. Your father was a very smart man.

EUGENE. You know Latin? *(She doesn't; He chuckles.)* Oh, you almost had me, you, you ... whipper-snapper!

BELLA. What does it mean?

EUGENE. Well, you know, you have a whip, and you snap it. *(Makes whipping motion.)* You know- a whipper, snapper.

BELLA. No, no, the Latin stuff.

EUGENE. Oh, ah. It translates to: "Exception confirms the rule in the cases not excepted."

BELLA. Ooooh, yeah. Totally agree.

EUGENE. Are you just agreeing to be agreeable?

BELLA. I need you to love me.

EUGENE. Well, what he's basically saying is there are certain rules in life - ways that just are. And then, without fail, there's exceptions to those rules. Special cases, you know ... like when it's always a certain way, except when it's not. Like a bird that can't fly! Or, or free parking on Sundays.

BELLA. I see ... oh! Oh! Like a penguin?!

EUGENE. Yes, exactly like a penguin.

BELLA. Eugene, are you saying I'm exactly like a

penguin? 'Cuz that would be awesome.

EUGENE. Sometimes life is funny, that's all I'm saying. You just ... you never know. *(A moment. Suzanne returns with a fresh martini.)*

SUZANNE. Okay my little chickadees, what in St. Paul Jerome's name is going on in here? We should be dancing! ¡Vamos a bailar! *(Let's dance!)* Alexa, play "Suzie's Sexy Mix"! *(Music plays. Bella drags Eugene to his feet. After brief dancing, Suzanne lowers the music.)* You know, ya little pooper-scoopers, ya got me thinking. Lots of deep thoughts in this pretty little head.

BELLA. Tell us all your pretty little head thoughts!

EUGENE. A general synopsis will do.

SUZANNE. So, I'm thinking- y'all were adopted- rescued, or whatnot, right?

BELLA. Oh, yes! I was crying in my kennel; then Bobby saw me and I saw him, and we saw each other!

SUZANNE. So that means Charlotte and Robert had to like, choose you. Take you into their homes, not knowing what that would be like ... I mean, if that's not love, then ... I just don't know what is. Accepting something, taking care of it ... even if it has like psycho-trauma issues, or pukes all over your new Jimmy Choos.

BELLA. Bobby's so good to me.

SUZANNE. I can't even keep my manicure alive.

BELLA. I throw up on his stuff all the time.

SUZANNE. Well, enough of the mooshy stuff. C'mon, smoochy-poochies, I love this song! Alexa, volume eleven! *(The music volume increases and all dance wildly around the room, enjoying themselves. Yes, even Eugene. Robert and Charlotte enter. Everyone stops, shocked. The music is paused.)*

CHARLOTTE. What the heck is going on in here?!

BELLA. We love each other!

EUGENE. I don't know who I am anymore. *(He goes to his corner.)*

CHARLOTTE. Suzanne, what is happening? *(Suzanne is somewhere making herself small, drinking her martini. Bella runs to Robert.)*

BELLA. Bobby!

ROBERT. Hey, Bella baby. How ya doin?

BELLA. Everything is wonderful! Eugene and I are basically in love, but like, best friend love. Grouchy old man, adorable me kind of love!

CHARLOTTE. Eugene, are you okay?

EUGENE. The question is you okay, Charlotte. Are you. Oh. Kay.

CHARLOTTE. I don't understand. What is going on with you?

EUGENE. Well I could ask you the same thing, you know. I could ask you that question, too. *(Pause. Embraces Charlotte.)* Charlotte, never leave me again!

CHARLOTTE. Suzanne! This is unacceptable.

SUZANNE. What? Who?

EUGENE. No, Charlotte, you are unacceptable! Oh, no - I mean, exceptional. *(Blinks.)* You are an exceptional woman, Charlotte.

CHARLOTTE. *(Spots Eugene's glass.)* Suzanne, is my dog drunk? *(Eugene goes to speak, mutters. Moves to a comfy spot on the floor.)*

SUZANNE. Sweetheart, this … *(Gestures to everything.)* … is all just a metaphor. To show you … to show what it's like … to illustrate to you … life.

CHARLOTTE. I can't believe this.

ROBERT. Honey, it's all good. They made a mess; we'll clean it up.

CHARLOTTE. Suzanne, I asked you to do one thing: to check on the dogs, make sure they weren't destroying each other, or the house!

SUZANNE. Yes.

CHARLOTTE. And the house is destroyed! You're destroyed, my dog is destroyed. This is complete destruction!

EUGENE. Whoa. Whoa. Charlotte. This is not yourself. This is not you. You are not you.

BELLA. How can I help?

CHARLOTTE. You! Shush your squeaking.

ROBERT. Charlotte!

BELLA. Bobby!

EUGENE. Oh, this, this is not good. Please, Charlotte, come seat down. *(Pats seat beside him.)*

CHARLOTTE. This is my house. I can't come home to this!

ROBERT. Hey, hey, come sit down, take a deep breath. We're all okay. We'll get it cleaned up.

SUZANNE. Yeah, baby-girl, we'll get this taken care of.

CHARLOTTE. But I don't want to clean it up!

SUZANNE. Okay, okay, I gotchu. *(She begins to clean up the mess; Everyone watches. It's a pathetic attempt.)*

CHARLOTTE. No! *(To Suzanne.)* You. Out of my house.

SUZANNE. Charlotte, sweetie pants.

BELLA. Charlotte, let her stay!

ROBERT. Hey now, Charlotte.

CHARLOTTE. Everyone stop saying my name! I am not a child and this is my home. *(To Suzanne.)* And you may leave it.

SUZANNE. Okay, I hear you, I do. Let me just ... grab my things. *(Dramatically collects her things; goes to door, turns.)* You know, it seems to me, chickie-poo, you may wanna get used to cleaning up other people's messes, if you know what I know that I know what you mean that I mean. *(She gives Charlotte a pointed look; dramatically exits.)*

ROBERT. What was that?

CHARLOTTE. My God, can she like smell it on me or something? Do I exude some special scent?

EUGENE. You do smell exceptionally wonderful lately, Charlotte. Like a cinnamon bun warming in the oven.

BELLA. Mmm, cinnamon buns.

CHARLOTTE. Oh my God, I can barely take care of a dog, and now, and now -

ROBERT. And now everything is fine!

BELLA. Everything is so fine! Suzanne told us all about being a flower but really a potato, and Eugene danced around like a pretty ballerina -

ROBERT. Bella, please, go sit. They were just having fun. Sure, maybe it got a little out of hand - and you're probably clear out of liquor - but it's nothing we can't handle.

CHARLOTTE. Maybe I don't want to handle it. Maybe I don't want to come home to, to chaos! It's not healthy, it's not safe, and you know what? When I really think about it, Eugene never exhibited any of these behaviors until Bella here came along.

BELLA. Say what?

EUGENE. Ding ding ding!

ROBERT. Um, where is this coming from?

CHARLOTTE. From your precious Maltese, apparently.

ROBERT. Seriously? Did you not just see the same scene I saw? Oh, but yeah, Bella's the one throwing the party.

CHARLOTTE. Robert!

ROBERT. What, Charlotte? No, I'm sorry, but you're pointing the finger at Bella like she's some sneaky conspirator. She's a stupid puppy, for God's sake!

BELLA. *(Wanting everyone happy.)* I'm just a stupid puppy!

CHARLOTTE. I don't know what to say. We were at dinner, and it was great, and you make me laugh, so much - you really make me so happy, but now my house is a mess and my head is a mess, and she knows, and your dog is glaring at me and I just don't know what to say!

ROBERT. Bella is not glar- *(Spots Bella.)* Bella, stop.

CHARLOTTE. I'm finding it hard to breathe.

ROBERT. Charlotte, hey, it's okay.

EUGENE. Hard to breathe!? Charlotte, that is not okay. *(To Robert.)* Don't tell her that's okay. *(Charlotte reclines on couch, as before. Eugene joins.)* Ooh, we're doing this again.

BELLA. Bobby, what are they doing?

ROBERT. Um, Charlotte?

EUGENE. Just breathe, Charlotte. In, out...

BELLA. Oh! Oh! I wanna breathe, too! *(She eagerly joins the upside-down couch party.)*

ROBERT. Okay, this is freaking me out a little here.

CHARLOTTE. I just feel so ... *(Incomprehensible sounds /words.)*

EUGENE. I understand, Charlotte. Emotions are ugly, despicable things; I recommend repressing them.

CHARLOTTE. *(Calmed; speaking clearly now.)* Robert, why did you bring me that plant?

ROBERT. What plant?

CHARLOTTE. That plant.

ROBERT. Well, because- I told you, I thought you might like it, you and Eugene. And I thought ... I thought it might be a nice way to mark this step in our relationship.

BELLA. Eugene's already marked it.

CHARLOTTE. *(Disembarks the couch.)* Well, did you consider maybe I wouldn't want that sort of responsibility? It's a living thing, you know. A living thing you just waltzed into my home and handed to me and now I have to take care of it and keep it alive so it doesn't die.

ROBERT. Well, I ... I didn't really think ...

CHARLOTTE. No, you didn't. *(Pause.)* I can't do this anymore.

ROBERT. Do what?

CHARLOTTE. This. Us. You and me.

ROBERT. Um, I must've blacked out there for a second because this feels like it's coming out of nowhere.

CHARLOTTE. We only just met each other, and it's way too soon.

ROBERT. For our dogs to meet?

CHARLOTTE. For all of it. All of it. All the things.

ROBERT. We've been dating for almost a year, Charlotte.

CHARLOTTE. Okay, yeah, and what do you really know about me?

ROBERT. I'd like to think I know a helluva lot.

EUGENE. *(Snorts.)* What you know about this fascinating woman could fit into the small end of a stick.

CHARLOTTE. Well, well ... do you know that I

sometimes wear the same socks two days in a row?

ROBERT. No, but that's ... not really ... a problem -

CHARLOTTE. And that occasionally I'll wake up in the middle of the night and eat ice cream like a starving little mouse -

EUGENE. Yeah, that's pretty adorable.

BELLA. I like ice cream.

ROBERT. I mean, that's actually kind of cute -

CHARLOTTE It's not cute! None of this is cute. I'm not some magical creature come into your life made of sunshine and rainbows and just puking up cute, sunshiny things.

ROBERT. I never thought -

CHARLOTTE. You did. You think I'm great. And tidy and together and disciplined like a damn butler and apparently perfect. Well ... *(Looks, knocks something over.)* I'm not! See?

EUGENE. *(Promptly fixes the upturned item.)* Charlotte, I mean really.

ROBERT. Okay, okay ... maybe I don't know everything about you, and I don't know where the butler thing's coming from, but that's okay! We can still have a great life together.

CHARLOTTE. But how can you possibly know if you want a life with someone that you don't even possibly know?

ROBERT. What? That doesn't make a whole lotta ... Nope, never mind! I just want to, okay? I want to know everything about you.

CHARLOTTE. No, you don't. You'll find stuff that, I don't know, but you'll find things you don't like, and ... It just seems like perfect is a long way to fall.

ROBERT. Is that what's bothering you? Do you think I have some impossible standards for you or something?

CHARLOTTE. Maybe? I don't know. No. I'm sorry, I'm all over the place. Robert, there's something we need to talk about-

ROBERT. Charlotte, you will never disappoint me.

CHARLOTTE. What? Are we in the same room having this conversation? Robert, of course I will! I'll disappoint you, like, all the time - and you will disappoint me - you'll be a big, stupid disappointment.

ROBERT. Okay ...

CHARLOTTE. And we'll disappoint each other, all the time. Be serious.

EUGENE. You rarely, if ever, disappoint me, Charlotte. I think you're overre-

CHARLOTTE. And don't tell me I'm overreacting! I'm being serious.

EUGENE. Sorry.

ROBERT. I can see that. Listen, I get that you like a tidy place, but I mean, life gets messy sometimes -

CHARLOTTE. I mean, did you even bring Bella to those classes?

ROBERT. What classes?

CHARLOTTE Okay. The classes I got you when you brought her home - the obedience training, same place I brought Eugene.

EUGENE. Were you aware I was their star student? My picture is on display by their front -

CHARLOTTE. So? Did you?

ROBERT. Charlotte, things got busy, but we will, I promise-

CHARLOTTE. No, Robert, that's not good enough-

ROBERT. Hey, whatever this is really about, let's talk about it –

CHARLOTTE. No. This clearly isn't going to work. You need to leave. *(She crosses her arms, gestures to door. Eugene joins, mimics.)*

ROBERT. So we're kicking everybody out? Can't handle the conversations so we're just kicking everyone out?

BELLA. Bobby, let's go. Charlotte's sad. *(To Charlotte.)* I'm sorry if I upset you and you're super pretty and your house smells like flowers ... and I love you.

EUGENE. Didn't you hear the lady? Get out of our house!

BELLA. Your house smells like flowers but you smell like farts!

ROBERT. Bella, stop it! Stop it right now. Let's go. *(To Charlotte.)* I don't get it. I thought we were happy.

BELLA. We were so happy!

EUGENE. We were never happy, you street urchin.

ROBERT. Charlotte, what are we doing? Let's choose happiness.

EUGENE. Happiness is not possible!

CHARLOTTE. Just stop it, Eugene! Stop it! Go to your bed! Robert, I don't know what you want me to say! You dropped the ball. I was afraid we weren't ready and obviously I was right.

ROBERT. Yeah, seems like you're making pretty darn sure of that.

CHARLOTTE. And what is that supposed to mean?

BELLA. Bobby is the bestest!

CHARLOTTE. Tell your dog to be quiet!

BELLA. Fine!

ROBERT. Tell your dog to get over himself!

CHARLOTTE. Fine!

EUGENE. *(Petulantly.)* I will not!

ROBERT. Bella, let's go.

CHARLOTTE. Robert, just wait, I think we need to -

ROBERT. No, I won't "just wait". I came here with an idea of where we are, who we are, but I see that we're not.

CHARLOTTE. Oh?

ROBERT. That's very clear to me right now.

CHARLOTTE. Oh.

ROBERT. I love you. I know you know that. And this is not the way I hoped this evening would go - like, not even close. But I won't be told what to do as though I don't have a say in what our life gets to look like. So yeah, Bella and I are leaving, and that's fine. C'mon, Bells. Goodbye, Eugene. Charlotte. *(Robert and Bella exit.)*

EUGENE. *(Awkward pause.)* Well. Good riddance, am I right?

CHARLOTTE. Be quiet, Eugene.

EUGENE. Okay.

CHARLOTTE. *(Sits on the couch; pats the couch cushion.)* C'mon. *(Eugene joins Charlotte. A beat, then Bella bursts back through the door.)*

BELLA. But, Eugene, what if it's me?! What if it's like you said, and we exceptio probat and spit in the standard's face!?

EUGENE. You are not making any sense.

BELLA. Oh, silly bear, you and me! Me and you! Maybe ... maybe we're the penguin to the rule. *(Beat. Robert returns.)*

ROBERT. Sorry, Charlotte. C'mon, Bells.

BELLA. *(Runs out the door with Robert.)* Think about it,

Eugie! Bestest, bestest friends!

CHARLOTTE. Robert, I need to tell you something - *(Door closes. Charlotte is stunned. Long pause.)*

EUGENE. *(Clears his throat.)* Well, good riddance, am I right?

CHARLOTTE. What is wrong with you? Look at our house, Eugie. You have never acted this way.

EUGENE. I was just trying to protect us ...

CHARLOTTE. Go. Go to your room. Go to your bed. *(Eugene remains; hurt.)* Go! Get out of here! I don't want to see you anymore! *(Eugene exits. Charlotte cleans; throws something, collapses amongst the rubble, sobbing. Eugene returns.)*

EUGENE. Charlotte, I can not remain in this state of emotional turmoil! Conversate with me! *(Spots Charlotte.)* Oh ... *(A knock at the door.)*

SUZANNE. Yoo-hoo! Charlotte-poo! *(She sneaks an arm in; drops her purse.)*

EUGENE. Never mind, interpersonal conflict is fine with me! *(Eugene expediently exits. Suzanne enters.)*

SUZANNE. Charlotte, my little harlot! I know you told me to leave, but I forgot- my purse! And that just won't do. *(Spots Charlotte.)* Oh. Oh, my. Well, yes. Life is hard and love is harder. I hear ya, dollface, I do. *(Grabs purse, goes to leave.)* Okay, thank you! Leaving now ...

CHARLOTTE. Suzanne! He's gone and it's all my fault!

SUZANNE. What we talking about, sweetums? That hunka hunka burning man? Did you scare him away? Well, of course you did — you were huffing and puffing everything all to bits, you know. I've never seen you like that. Or like this.

CHARLOTTE. I've never felt this way! It's like I'm

bursting with love, so there I go and ruin everything. You want something, you know, and then there it is, right in front of you, so of course I just piss all over it!

SUZANNE. Like owner, like dog.

CHARLOTTE. I'm going to be alone forever!

SUZANNE. Oh, sugar tits, that's never gonna happen. If not him, someone else will snatch you up and love you silly.

CHARLOTTE. But I don't want anybody else!

SUZANNE. Okay, fine, I'll bite. Why him and only him?

CHARLOTTE Because he's good to me, Suzie, and he makes me laugh. And he pushes me outside my comfortable neurotic box. And he encourages me - our very first date, he said to me ... he said I reminded him of his junior high librarian -

SUZANNE. Okay, that's a little weird -

CHARLOTTE. 'Cuz she was smart and cute, Suzanne - smart and cute!

SUZANNE. Okay, okay! Darlin, this is not the end. We always think it's the end, but it's almost never the end.

CHARLOTTE. Do you, do you think you and Alejandro will get back together?

SUZANNE. Oh, no sweetie, that's the end. Charlotte, you're a sweetheart and we're all entitled to our own personal psychodramas.

CHARLOTTE. I'm sorry for speaking to you like that, like before.

SUZANNE. Honey, it was a thrill to be reprimanded by you. *(Eugene returns, deescalating from his antics but still a little affected by it all.)*

EUGENE. Charlotte! I'm back. Okay, there you are. We really must talk. You and me. Look at me! Look at me.

SUZANNE. And I never meant to get your dog drunk.

CHARLOTTE. Oh, Eugie. I'm sorry, I never asked - did you have a good day?

EUGENE. It was a wonderful day and the very recollection of its wonderfulness disgusts me.

CHARLOTTE. There, there, buddy. You miss Bella?

EUGENE. What? Ew. No. Puke. Gross.

SUZANNE. Hey, um, dog. Eugene, I'm sorry. I shoulda taken better care of ya.

EUGENE. You were just having fun. I was trying to have fun too. But it hurt me.

CHARLOTTE. You trying to say something, Eugie?

EUGENE. Having fun physically and emotionally hurts me! But enough of that. Bobbert, Bobby - that guy. He's pretty great. Okay, no, he's tolerable. And the perky, melodramatic thing - she's acceptable. I could accept having them here all the time. Some of the time. Occasionally. Oh, just go get 'em, Tiger!

CHARLOTTE. Got a lot on your mind, don'tcha, darlin'?

SUZANNE. Is he, like, really talking to you?

CHARLOTTE. Of course he is! Aren'tcha, buddy?

EUGENE. Well, I'm certainly not talking to myself.

SUZANNE. Like ... you actually understand what he's saying?

CHARLOTTE. *(Pause.)* Suzanne. That's just silly.

SUZANNE. Oh yeah, yeah - no, of course. It's just ... you're all like ... meeting of the minds, and all.

CHARLOTTE. Well, we just understand each other, don't we, Eugie?

EUGENE. I feel sometimes you're missing key points, but overall, yes. *(A knock at the door)* What's that? *(Another knock.)* Ah-ha! It is the musical cadence of the conquistador's measured gait as he marches off into glorious battle! *(He gallops, wanders to corner, lies down.)*

SUZANNE. Well, are ya gonna answer the door, sweetums, or we gonna sit here watching your dog convulse about in a delirious stupor? I mean, seriously, this can't all be my fault.

CHARLOTTE. Okay, okay. I got this. Oh, and Suzanne, that important thing I wanted to talk to you about ...

SUZANNE. Yes, of course, you're pregnant.

CHARLOTTE. What?

SUZANNE. I'm clairvoyant, naturally.

CHARLOTTE. But how did you? Because I only just -

ROBERT. *(Offstage.)* Charlotte, will you please let me in? *(Suzanne gestures. Charlotte, flustered, opens the door. Robert enters as Suzanne hides.)* I'm sorry, Charlotte, but I cannot and will not leave things this way.

CHARLOTTE. You came back.

ROBERT. I never left. I mean, not really. I was in the parking lot, wondering what to say, what to do.

CHARLOTTE. You never really left.

EUGENE. Good heavens it's Robert Bobbert! Hey – Charlotte – look - there he is! You went and got him! Jolly good.

ROBERT. Can you please shut him up?

CHARLOTTE. Eugene, please be quiet.

EUGENE. Well, I never ... *(He returns to lie down.)*

ROBERT. You don't get to just have your say, kick me out, and be done with it. I have feelings too, you know.

SUZANNE. *(Appears.)* And you're about to have a few more, Bobby!

ROBERT. *(Startled, but then calms himself.)* Oh, you're here.

SUZANNE. I'm feeling things, too, Bobby. Especially now you've barged in on such a manly mission, whacking piñatas around, looking for sweet, sweet candy.

ROBERT. I didn't realize you were here.

SUZANNE. Oh, I'm here. Pay me no mind. *(Steps back.)* Pay me no mind.

ROBERT. *(To Charlotte.)* Why is she here?

SUZANNE. *(Steps forward.)* She is here because her friend is in emotional angst, and that is what a friend does. I embrace my friend's turmoil and I create something new; I transform it. And because - Bobby - I told you if you ever hurt Charlotte I would get all messy up in this place, and now I feel like the time has come ... for the mess.

CHARLOTTE. Oh, no, Suzanne, he didn't really do any -

ROBERT. You think I hurt her? Me? I hurt her. No, that's not how that went. Charlotte here decided to randomly reach in, rip out my heart, throw it on the ground - kinda stomp on it for a bit - then ask me to leave!

CHARLOTTE. It wasn't like that!

ROBERT. After months of learning about and falling in love with each other, I didn't even get a chance to have a conversation. You just kicked me out, threw me out like, like yesterday's crossword puzzle that you and your dog figured out in like five minutes -

CHARLOTTE. It takes us longer than five minutes, Robert-

ROBERT. Threw me out, just like you threw out Suzanne!

SUZANNE. *(Pause.)* Come to think of it, that didn't feel very good.

CHARLOTTE. Hey now, the two of you. It's not like that.

I needed some time to think.

SUZANNE. But your smelly dog creature got to stay.

ROBERT. Oh my God, I forgot Bella! Bella! *(He opens the door; Bella skips in, wearing her sweater.)*

BELLA. *(Singing.)* And all the fluffy piglets came swinging through the trees, and all I'm thinking is won't you come swing with me! *(Stops.)* Oh my goodness, where is Eugene? Is he here?

EUGENE. What, what, what?

BELLA. Eugene!! I have found thee! *(Eugene passes out.)* Come back to me, Eugene! Eugene!

CHARLOTTE. *(To Robert.)* It's your turn to shut up your dog.

ROBERT. My dog is adorable. Your dog is an asshole. *(*Option: "entitled jerk".)*

SUZANNE. Hold on! Okay, okay, everyone just hold on tightly to your tiny little pony horses. Bobby, are you here to make things nice with my little Charlotte-harlot?

ROBERT. Yes. She can't just get rid of me like -

SUZANNE. Yes, yes, thank you. And Charlotte, were you not just wailing like a be-headed banshee, screaming "Bobby - Bobby, come back to me, Bobby!"

ROBERT. What's this?

CHARLOTTE. I was absolutely not ... doing those things.

SUZANNE. *(Puts arms around them.)* So, what I'm seeing here, is an opportunity. A catalyst for communication. I do believe my friend Freud would have a few thoughts to share with you on the subject.

ROBERT. Wait, what?

SUZANNE. He can't be here right now, but I'm willing to share my insights in his stead. A little couple's sesh, if you please.

CHARLOTTE. I don't know if that's necessary-

ROBERT. Oh, no, we don't -

SUZANNE. All right, all right, here we go. I'm highly trained. Charlotte, you stand here. And Bobby, my burly burrito of a man, you can be here. Now! Here we go. I shall recline, as such ... *(Freudian.)* and now I will ask you a few questions ...

ROBERT. I'm pretty sure we're the ones who are supposed to lie on the couch.

SUZANNE. Is that the way this goes, Bobby? That's not the way this goes! Hold on, I'm dizzy. Okay. Now, here we are.

ROBERT. Charlotte -

SUZANNE. Let me conduct the session, Robert!

ROBERT. Can we please just talk? *(He takes a step forward; Suzanne stops him with her foot.)*

SUZANNE. Quiet, Bobby! Stay in your spot. Now, Charlotte, what was it you wished to say to Robert while you were rolling back and forth on your condo floor howling like a distressed hyena?

CHARLOTTE. I wasn't really - it wasn't that bad - I just, okay. Robert, I wish I had been more clear with you.

ROBERT. Well, I wish you had been, too -

SUZANNE. Hey - manly man. Let the lady speak. *(To Charlotte.)* You may speak.

CHARLOTTE. Thank you. *(To Robert.)* I'm scared you'll get to know me, you know, things about me, and you won't like the way I am. I can be so ... harsh, and particular, and Robert, you're so understanding and patient and I know that can't last forever. *(Pause.)* But I see now maybe I'm not giving you enough credit. Or myself, for that matter. I can be very lovable.

SUZANNE. You are, you are. So much truth in those words, so much insight. So, I'm hearing that you're scared. And Bobby here represents new territory, perhaps territory that's just too expansive, and you're afraid to explore it without the proper climbing gear. I hear ya, I do. Now, Bobby, your turn. Tell Charlotte how you feel, how you feel inside your heart.

ROBERT. Okay ... Well, um, let me see - I don't feel like we need to be having this conversation with a kimono-clad lady-friend of yours guiding the way -

SUZANNE. *(Freudian.)* Stick to ze facts!

ROBERT. Those are the facts!

SUZANNE. Stick to the feelings, then! The feelings you have for Charlotte.

ROBERT. Fine! Fine, I'm scared, too, okay? I'm scared I'm not the kind of man you'll stay interested in forever. I'm scared next week you'll be checking out a book at that pillared library you designed and someone will have something witty to say and you'll realize I'm an idiot. Mostly, I'm afraid you enjoy sudoku with your dog better than an actual conversation with me. Okay? Okay, Suzanne? You happy now?

SUZANNE. Bobbert, my happiness is of no import to this particular scenario. Charlotte? Responses, feedback, hmm?

CHARLOTTE. I should've been more vulnerable with you. And I should've let you talk. Robert, you're constantly surprising me.

ROBERT. Look, I'm not going anywhere - I mean, unless you actually want me to -

CHARLOTTE. I don't. I really, really don't.

ROBERT. And I don't think you're perfect; I don't want you to be. Also, I'm sorry what I said about your dog.

CHARLOTTE. And I'm sorry I said that about Bella.

She's incredible.

BELLA. So much truth in those words.

ROBERT. I'm stuck on you, Charlotte. You ain't getting rid of me that easy. *(Suzanne gazes at Robert and Charlotte as they gaze at each other. Her job is now done.)*

SUZANNE. Well. From the lava-like embers in y'all's eyeballs it's about to get warm in here. However, before I go, I believe there's still something important Charlotte would like to share with the class.

CHARLOTTE. Oh, Suzanne, no-

SUZANNE. No, yourself. You can't leave little white sticks laying about and divulge intense personal confessions before opening doors to burly burrito man and expect me to just sit on it. With all due respect.

CHARLOTTE. But we don't need to talk about this right now-

SUZANNE. Oh, but we do -

CHARLOTTE. Oh, but we don't -

ROBERT. Oh, but what are we talking about ?

SUZANNE. You see, Bobby, our charlatan Charlotte here has been keeping something from us, keeping it to herself like a little squirrelly squirrel hoarding away her little squirrel nuts.

ROBERT. I don't ... understand ...

SUZANNE. Well, I think it is vitally important that you know that our little Charlotte here is in fact quite -

CHARLOTTE. *(Pushes Suzanne towards the door.)* Quite grateful for all your assistance, Suzie! You are truly a gifted and insightful relationship counselor.

SUZANNE. *(Flattered.)* Oh, why, yes. Yes, this is true.

CHARLOTTE. And now you're leaving.

SUZANNE. *(To Robert.)* I'm highly trained, you know.

CHARLOTTE. Yes, and we thank you for that. For all you do for us.

SUZANNE. So many things.

CHARLOTTE. Yes, thank you! *(She goes to shut the door; Suzanne stops her.)*

SUZANNE. Wait, wait, wait! Before I go! Something important.

CHARLOTTE. Please, Suzanne, just let me -

SUZANNE. *(Dramatically.)* I must confer ... with the Shih-Tzu!

CHARLOTTE. Who?

BELLA. *(Perks up.)* Wait, you mean me?

ROBERT. You mean Bella? She's a Maltese.

SUZANNE. Yes, with the poodle. Come here, fluffernutter. *(Suzanne and Bella converge; suddenly dizzy.)* Oh, okay, still a little topsy-turvy. Perhaps we should sit. You see, Belladonna, I couldn't leave without discussing one more thing with you.

CHARLOTTE. Um, Suzie -

SUZANNE. Please don't interfere, Charlotte.

CHARLOTTE. Okay ... *(Backs off.)*

SUZANNE. So, as we were saying earlier, about you being adopted or whatnot, rescued. I've been wondering if ... if I could ever be accepted like that, you know? Taken in, all my flaws, and loved.

BELLA. Well, Suzie. Sometimes it feels like it's never gonna happen ... but then it does. Someone sees you, they just see you, and they say - "There you are!".

SUZANNE. This is not the end.

BELLA. Everything always gets better. Not all at once,

but slowly, like a sunrise.

SUZANNE. You are a wonderful comfort, little fluffy creature.

CHARLOTTE. You're aware, Suzanne, that you don't even like dogs?

SUZANNE. Charlotte, please keep your insensitive comments to yourself, thank you. Thank you, Belladonna. *(Heads to door, pauses.)* You know, dancing with you dogs was better than any dance with Alejandro. I wasn't worried about my hair, or what you were thinking, probably because your brains are like this big. But you saw me, you know? And it had nothing to do with the way I looked.

BELLA. The way Bobby saw me.

ROBERT. I have to admit, they're pretty special -

SUZANNE. Your opinion on the subject is completely unnecessary, Bobby. I know, Freud knows, we all know how you feel about it. Well. This has been an experience. Charlotte, sweetie, you take care of you.

CHARLOTTE. Thank you for not ... forcing the subject.

SUZANNE. Well, it's not in my nature to force anything into this world. I prefer things to unfold naturally, you know what I mean Bobby? No? Okay. Au revoir! *(Sees herself in mirror.)* Oh, there you are. I am one sexy sweet potato. And you. *(To Charlotte.)* Better go check ya shrubbery. *(She dramatically exits.)*

ROBERT. Was that an innuendo about your -

CHARLOTTE. I don't know, but, Robert ...
(Together.) I have something important to tell you.

ROBERT. *(Together.)* I have something important to ask you.

CHARLOTTE. I'm so glad you came back -

ROBERT. Never left -

CHARLOTTE. Never left. I'll go make us a drink - you a drink. I'll make a drink. Stay here with the dogs?

ROBERT. Yeah, I can do that. *(Bella jumps to follow Charlotte.)*

CHARLOTTE. Stay here, Bella. Stay with Eugene. *(She exits to kitchen. Robert sits on couch; pulls out the ring. Bella remembers that Eugene is there and he's her best friend.)*

BELLA. Eugene!! You're missing all the fun!

EUGENE. What, huh? I was dreaming of a home ... peaceful and secure ... and Charlotte was there, feeding me peaches.

BELLA. Well, I'm here! Eugene, aren't you happy!? Aren't you happy happy happy!?

EUGENE. Yes, hello, Bella. You were there, too.

BELLA. In your dream? What was I doing? Was I dancing around and saving your life from a pirate parakeet with petunias?

EUGENE. What? No. No, you were just ... I don't know, there.

BELLA. With petunias?

EUGENE. Sure.

BELLA. Oh, that's wonderful. Did I save your life?

EUGENE. You did not. Isn't being there enough?

BELLA. It is. it really is. You're happy to see me. I can tell.

EUGENE. I highly doubt this feeling is happiness ... Wait a minute, maybe it is ...

BELLA. Ooh, what does it feel like, Eugie? Describe it to me.

EUGENE. Well, there's an odd little fluttering in my ... more like a ... Oh, God, I'm gonna be sick. Charlotte! *(Charlotte enters as Eugene runs to kitchen, hacking.)*

BELLA. Oh my gosh, Eugene - that's love! That feeling is love! *(Bella runs after Eugene, exits to kitchen.)*

CHARLOTTE. Oh no, I'll go check on them. One second, Robert. *(Charlotte exits; Bella returns.)*

BELLA. Eugene is sick and it's totally disgusting and I'm so glad you brought us here, Bobby! This is where we belong.

ROBERT. I'm gonna do it, Bells. I'm gonna ask her.

BELLA. Ask her what, Bobby? *(Robert shows Bella the ring)* Oooh, shiny!

ROBERT. What do you think? Too soon, after all this? What d'ya think?

BELLA. I think it's shiny. *(She goes to eat ring; Robert pulls away, chuckles.)*

ROBERT. People warned me about the shelters, you know. Said I might get some screwed up dog with issues ... *(Sounds of Eugene hacking in kitchen.)* ... but clearly I lucked out. Whatever your issues, Bella dog, we'd figure it out. *(Charlotte and Eugene enter; Robert hides the ring behind his back.)*

CHARLOTTE. I'm sorry, dear, one more minute. I'm just gonna get Eugene fixed up a bit.

EUGENE. Don't look at me. *(Charlotte and Eugene do the walk of shame, exit to bedroom hallway. Bella giggles.)*

BELLA. Eugene is silly.

ROBERT. Oh yeah, Bells? Gosh, before you came along, I was lonely - whatever, I'll admit it. But then I saw you. And I brought you home, and now every day I open that door and there you are, wiggling your butt, totally freakishly obsessed with me, and it just ... makes everything better.

BELLA. It really does.

ROBERT. I actually have no idea what I did before you.

BELLA. Aw, shucks Bobbert. I love you so much it hurts me like a lot! *(Looks closely at the ring.)* And I think it's shiny and I want to eat it. *(Bella goes to eat the ring as Robert stands; Bella falls over.)*

ROBERT. Charlotte, I have a question for you!

CHARLOTTE. *(Enters.)* Sorry. Ha! Here we are. *(Eugene enters, decked out in a new sweater. He is more himself - sober, uptight.)*

ROBERT. Lookin' good, Eugene!

EUGENE. Yes, well. Hello again.

BELLA. Hi, Eugene!

EUGENE. Yes, well. Hello again. *(He returns to his corner.)*

ROBERT. Charlotte, we need to talk.

CHARLOTTE. I know, I didn't mean to be so -

ROBERT. I lied to you, Charlotte. Wait! No, I lied to you because the fact is, you're right - I don't want to spend my life getting to know you. *(Bella gasps dramatically.)* Wait! No, that still didn't come out right. Come here. *(He tries to take her hand, but she resists.)*

CHARLOTTE. No, no, it's okay. I understand.

EUGENE. Maybe you should stop talking now, Bobbert.

BELLA. Yeah, that might be a good idea -

ROBERT. Charlotte! You are far too mysterious and complicated and beautiful and wonderful for me to ever fully understand you. That's what I was trying to say! And I love that I will never know everything about you. You'll keep surprising me, and I hope I keep surprising you! That's the way I want it. I want it that way, forever.

CHARLOTTE. Oh, Robert. I ... I don't know what to say.

ROBERT. Say yes.

BELLA. Yes! Say yes! Yes, yes, yes!

EUGENE. Wait, yes to what? There hasn't been a question. Charlotte, do not answer questions you have not yet been given.

CHARLOTTE. Robert, I lied to you, too.

ROBERT. What?

BELLA. What?

CHARLOTTE. By omission? Delay? By not telling you something I should have told you at the very beginning, before everything got way out of control.

ROBERT. Charlotte, what aren't you telling me?

CHARLOTTE. You see, I discovered something earlier, something that could potentially change everything we're doing here together ...

ROBERT. Charlotte, what aren't you telling me?

CHARLOTTE. I am telling you, right now. I am trying to tell you, right now. *(Pregnant pause.)* I'm pregnant.

EUGENE. What what what?!

ROBERT. Are you serious? Pregnant? As in, we're having a baby? You're serious right now? Oh my God- Bella, Bella, did ya hear that?

BELLA. Ahhhhh!!! *(Bella hugs Charlotte around the belly.)*

CHARLOTTE. Oh my gosh! Look, Robert, it's like she knows!

EUGENE. Well, yes, Charlotte, you did just inform us.

CHARLOTTE. *(To Robert.)* Are you okay?

ROBERT. Okay? I'm more than okay. Charlotte, we're having a baby!

CHARLOTTE. Yeah, we are.

BELLA. Eugie, did you hear that? We're having a baby!

EUGENE. Yes, yes, processing.

ROBERT. I mean, look at our success rate here - a thriving piece of plant shrubbery, check! Two dogs, check, check! My God, no wonder you were worried, Charlotte. Did you think I wouldn't be happy? I'm out of my mind happy about this. We're gonna be a family. So yeah? Does that mean we're a yes?

CHARLOTTE. Oh, Robert, of course- of course it's a yes!

ROBERT. I was hoping you'd say that. I was hoping you'd say that all day. *(He reaches into his pocket for the ring box.)*

CHARLOTTE. Oh Robert, you didn't!

ROBERT. I did, and it's awesome. I knew from the moment I saw you.

EUGENE. I know nothing of any of this. Why are we all behaving so cryptically?

BELLA. *(Singing.)* All the fluffy piglets in the world!

CHARLOTTE. But the dogs - they hadn't even met. Weren't you afraid everything would fall apart?

ROBERT. I guess I knew with enough hairspray we could just shellac us back together.

BELLA. Smoosh us together!

EUGENE. There will be no smooshing. Charlotte, can we please just take a nap?

ROBERT. *(Kneeling before Charlotte.)* Okay, Charlotte.

CHARLOTTE. Oh my gosh.

EUGENE. *(Stalks around, contemplates a coup.)* Oh, this

is nonsensical nugaciousness. First, it was Alfred, then that insipid creature and now this?

BELLA. Oh, you love me.

EUGENE. Irrelevant. And now an adorable baby child is growing in your womb - in your womb, Charlotte? And we're going to be a family? This is too much, too much all at once.

ROBERT. *(Stands, concerned.)* Eugene, buddy, you doing okay?

CHARLOTTE. Don't worry about him - he's fine. Focus on me.

EUGENE. Oh, I'm probably experiencing an acute myocardial infarction, but never mind me!

ROBERT. Charlotte, I will never understand you ... or your dog.

EUGENE. I am an enigma.

ROBERT. And I'll never know everything about you. But I do know *(Holds up ring box.)* this.

BELLA. Kiss her, Bobby!

EUGENE. Don't you dare touch her.

ROBERT. *(Returns to one knee.)* Charlotte, my dearest one ...

EUGENE. I say, sir, on your feet!

CHARLOTTE. Yes, Robert?

EUGENE. Stop communicating with him! He's a plague on both our houses!

CHARLOTTE. Eugene, would you please shut up? *(Eugene is horrified, but silent.)*

BELLA. *(Whispers.)* Just let them eat the shiny thing.

ROBERT. Charlotte. Will you marry me?

CHARLOTTE. Oh, Robert ... *(Before she can say yes,*

Eugene leaps over the couch.)

EUGENE. Balderdash and backgammon! This will not do! *(He grabs the ring; holds it up triumphantly.)*

ALL. Eugene, no! *(Eugene eats the shiny thing.)*

    Blackout.

END OF PLAY

PROPS LIST: (in order of use)

Crossword book(s) or Newspaper, Sudoku book(s) (set on stage)

Pregnancy stick (Charlotte)

Apron (Charlotte)

Fake (or real) plant/tree (Robert)

Ring in box (Robert)

Dog dish (Charlotte)

Sweater -for Bella (Robert)

Purse (Suzanne)

Bra (Eugene)

Hairbrush (Eugene)

Martini Glass (Suzanne)

Toy chest with dog toys and paraphernalia (set on stage)

Couch pillow- can be ripped apart/destroyed (set on stage)

Music Player / Alexa (set on stage)

Alcohol bottles (set on stage)

Drinking Glasses (set off stage, Suzanne & Charlotte)

NOTES

(Use this space to make notes for your production)

84

GATHER BY THE
GHOST LIGHT
ORIGINAL STORIES FOR RADIO THEATER

GATHER BY THE GHOST LIGHT is a storytelling podcast in radio theater format. Think of the Ghost Light as your campfire. Gather around and listen to stories from a variety of genres. Playwright Jonathan Cook and Devon McSherry are the hosts of the series and most of the stories you hear were originally written as short stage plays and they now have been adapted to audio plays with professional voice actors and immersive sound effects. The audio plays produced on this podcast give these talented playwrights an even wider audience for their stories. We welcome you to join us in this journey as we extend the voices of emerging playwrights!

Available wherever you get your podcasts!
For more information, please visit:
www.gatherbytheghostlight.com
YouTube@gatherbytheghostlight
Instagram@gatherbytheghostlight
Facebook@gatherbytheghostlight

HUGO SAVES CHRISTMAS…IN MAY!
by Steven Hayet

1M, 3W, COMEDY

For Maya Kaplan, Christmas is her life… and she hates every minute of it. As acting manager of the year-round Christmas store Yuletide Cheer, a job she reluctantly inherited after the owner (her mom) retired, Maya is force-fed jolly, subjected to hearing the same holiday songs on loop day after day. Fortunately, Maya's nightmare will be coming to an end in a few months as the store will finally shutter its doors to become a Starbucks. Or will it? Enter Hugo McGee, a longtime customer devastated to learn of the store's closing. Refusing to allow a local intuition to disappear, Hugo makes it his mission to raise the money and keep Yuletide Cheer open, despite Maya's objections.

KINGDUMB
by Jonathan Cook

10M, 6W, COMEDY

There's a new King in the land that has initiated a mysterious new tax on the citizens. Outraged, the region's finest Clock fixer, aka "Time Repair Specialist", recruits some of the most unlikely rebels to help him develop a plan to overthrow the King. Their plotting takes them on a comedic journey through perilous mountain tops all the way to the palace itself where they confront this vile King face to face. Kingdumb is a medieval fantasy comedy full of absurdist humor and illogical behavior.

BOBBY IS DEAD

by Marty Matfess

2M, 3W, DARK COMEDY

Chris has been madly in love with his best friend Annie for years, but she's only been interested in dating everyone else but him. After Annie's recent break up with her boyfriend Bobby, Chris feels this may finally be what he needs to find his way into her heart, but just like that ... she's already moved on to another guy she met at a coffee shop. Being the good friend that he is, Chris has agreed to hang out with the new guy's visiting sister while they go out on a date. Oh, and let's not forget about Bobby. Turns out he's not taking the breakup too well and Chris is now caught between an aggressive ex-boyfriend while having to keep new guy's sister company. A play about love, lust, and getting shot in the head.

IN THE SLUSH

by Daniel Prillaman

2M, 2W, HORROR

2023 FINALIST FOR NEW DRAMATISTS' PRINCESS GRACE AWARD

Newlywed Laura Beth Gardner has it all. A loving husband, a baby on the way, and a usually delightful job. But this weekend, tasked with reading through her publishing house's slush pile, she encounters a mysterious manuscript that claims she isn't human. That her husband isn't who he says he is. And that she's a vessel for her unborn child, who is actually the Second Coming of an ancient darkness that will devour the world. It has to be some sort of joke. …But what if it's not?

A cosmic horror about identity, creation, and the things we'll do to realize our dreams.